"As the door was thrust oper
Neal Larrard—calm and coc
ically, my fingers touched thc ___, __, _____ _ ___ _,_
did so, I felt that fearful dead thing pressing against my knees, and
felt also the muzzle of the revolver hard against my side."

The Girl Behind the Keys (1903) is a delightful early detective
novel in which Bella Thorn, a savvy and resourceful young
typist, foils the nefarious plans of her employer, a confidence
man who exploits the hopes and fears permeating the popular
imagination of his time.

With its urban setting and the immediacy of its sense of mal-
ice, *The Girl Behind the Keys* anticipates American hard-boiled
detective fiction of the 1930s and 1940s. Bella, in her coupling
of professional efficiency with almost uncanny instincts for
sniffing out mysteries, is a prototype of the girl Friday whose
assistance is vital to the success of the male investigator in many
early to mid-twentieth century detective stories.

Originally published as the Victorian era was giving way to modernity, *The Girl Behind the Keys* dramatizes society's alarm over
new knowledge and technologies. This tension, pervasive during
the period, simmers beneath the comic surface of the novel.

Tom Gallon (1866-1914) began to write short stories after illness
forced him to give up a clerical career. He went on to write over
forty novels, six plays, and numerous music hall sketches.

Arlene Young is Associate Professor of English at the University
of Manitoba. She is the author of *Culture, Class and Gender in the
Victorian Novel* (Palgrave Macmillan, 1999) and the editor of the
Broadview edition of *The Odd Women*, by George Gissing (1998).

THE GIRL BEHIND THE KEYS

Tom Gallon

edited by Arlene Young

broadview encore editions

Library and Archives Canada Cataloguing in Publication

Gallon, Tom, 1866-1914
    The girl behind the keys / Tom Gallon ; edited by Arlene Young.

(Broadview encore editions)
Includes bibliographical references.
ISBN 1-55111-473-9

I. Young, Arlene, 1948- II. Title. III. Series.
PR6013.A34G57 2005   823'.8   C2005-905022-5

Broadview Press, Ltd. Is an independent, international publishing house, incorporated in 1985. Broadview believes in shared ownership, both with its employees and with the general public; since the year 2000 Broadview shares have traded publicly on the Toronto Venture Exchange under the symbol BDP

We welcome any comments and suggestions regarding any aspect of our publication—please feel free to contact us at the addresses below, or at broadview@broadviewpress.com

Copy editor: Rebecca Conolly

North America
PO Box 1243, Peterborough, Ontario, Canada K9J 7H5
Tel: (705) 743-8990; Fax: (705) 743-8353; e-mail: customerservice@broadviewpress.com
PO Box 1015, 3576 California Road, Orchard Park, NY, USA 14127

UK, Ireland, and continental Europe
NBN Plymbridge
Estover Road
Plymouth PL6 7PY UK
Tel: 44 (0) 1752 202 301
Fax: 44 (0) 1752 202 331
Fax Order Line: 44 (0) 1752 202 333
Customer Service: cservs@nbnplymbridge.com
Orders: orders@nbnplymbridge.com

Australia and New Zealand
UNIREPS, University of New South Wales Sydney, NSW, 2052
Tel: 61 2 9664 0999; Fax: 61 2 9664 5420
e-mail: info.press@unsw.edu.au

www.broadviewpress.com

Typesetting by Aldo Fierro

Broadview Press Ltd. Gratefully acknowledges the financial support of the Government of Canada through the Book Publishing Industry Development Program for our publishing activities.

PRINTED IN CANADA

Contents

Acknowledgements

I wish to thank Natalie Johnson for her comments and her help in preparing this edition. I wish also to thank my daughter, Jennifer O'Kell, and my husband, Robert O'Kell, for indulging my enthusiasms for old technologies and seemingly inconsequential fiction.

Introduction

THE GIRL BEHIND THE KEYS AND ITS
CULTURAL AND LITERARY CONTEXTS

Although largely forgotten by all but detective story aficiona-
dos and scholars interested in women's work at the turn of the
last century,[1] *The Girl Behind the Keys* is one of those delightful gems of popular literature that, without any pretensions to
greatness and without losing any of the charm and lightness
of inconsequential fiction, manages to bring together a host
of the cultural and literary motifs that mark a particular his-
torical moment. That moment is 1903—the Victorian era is
barely gone and certainly not forgotten; the New Woman,[2]
a carry-over from the previous decade, continues to assert
her independence; modernity is an established phenomenon,
yet still recent enough to be novel; the technologies that will
transform daily life in the new century, such as electricity and
telephones, are already altering the workplace. Countering the
scientific sophistication of the period is a continuing popular
fascination with spiritualism, seances, and mediums. Detective
fiction, which will become the most popular of popular genres
in the twentieth century, is at the end of its formative stage,
with the most successful fictional sleuth of all time, Sherlock
Holmes, still in his prime. Into this world walks Bella Thorn,

---

[1]   Feminist historian Meta Zimmeck, for example, mentions it in "Jobs for the Girls:
      The Expansion of Clerical Work for Women, 1850-1914."
[2]   The literary-cum-social phenomenon of the New Woman dates from about 1883,
      with the publication of Olive Schreiner's *The Story of an African Farm*. Subsequent
      New Woman novels proliferated in the 1890s, as did commentary in the periodical
      press about the New Woman as a social type.

the eponymous girl behind the keys, who unites in her person and her story this strange mix of cultural and literary characteristics that merge the new-fangled and the old-fashioned in provocative and often humorous ways.

Bella is attractive, independent, and skilled at using the technology that transformed the nineteenth-century business office into the twentieth-century one—the typewriter; she is the virtual embodiment of modernity, the savvy young career woman at home in the urban landscape, a type that will become more prevalent as the twentieth century progresses. The story itself, however, betrays its peculiarly Victorian roots in its tendency to connect new technologies with mystery and the supernatural, a characteristic late nineteenth-century cultural response to technical innovations such as electricity, telephones, and typewriters. By the early twentieth century, these technologies had advanced to the point where they were not entirely unfamiliar to most people. Workable models for both the telephone and the typewriter were developed in the 1870s; in the 1880s and 1890s, they became fairly commonplace as business machines, although Britain was slow to adopt the telephone by comparison with North America. Telephones and typewriters were accordingly not likely to be found in the homes of ordinary people—the white- and blue-collar workers of the period—but were nevertheless changing the way many people lived their lives or defined who they were, particularly because these technologies were transforming office work by creating new opportunities and limiting old ones. The typist, for example, was replacing the copy clerk; the telephone made the message boy obsolete. In her fascinating study of technology at the turn of the last century, *When Old Technologies Were New*,

Carolyn Marvin analyzes part of this phenomenon, specifically the development of the expert (the electrician, the engineer) as part of an elite. Marvin traces the development of new social power networks, along with the new communication networks. Bella is lower down this power grid—she is a cog rather than a wheel, a member of the socially disenfranchised lower middle class, who nevertheless carves out for herself a niche of individual expression, personal liberty, even of power. Bella is able to exploit one of the less obvious effects of technology at the *fin de siècle*—the subtle disruption of power networks at the level of social interaction. Bella may be subordinate to her unscrupulous employers, but they are in turn dependent upon her superior grasp of technology.

The technological expertise that empowers Bella is, of course, her knowledge of the typewriter and typing. While the idea of the manual typewriter as mystifying technology may seem odd to us in the twenty-first century, at the turn of the last century the average person was uninformed about its operation. Indeed, so mystifying was the typewriter to most people that writers were able to play with the idea of connecting typewriters with the supernatural. Like "The Spirit of Sarah Keech" episode in *The Girl Behind the Keys*, a number of stories from that period associate typewriters with automatic writing, or spirit-writing. One of these, "Mr. Twistleton's Type-Writer," which appeared in *Cornhill Magazine* in 1887, is unusual in that it casts a professional man—the Mr. Twistleton of the title, who is a successful barrister—as the typist. He is a comic character, but he is also portrayed as a man of stern character who is utterly devoted both to his wife and to the typewriter that he has taught himself to use with a high level of proficiency. His two weaknesses—his possessiveness of both wife and typewriter and his belief in ghosts—lead to the comic dilemma occasioned when his coveted machine starts producing messages that question the faithfulness of his wife. Twistleton's conviction that the machine is haunted has him placing more credence in its mystical powers than in his wife's integrity, a comic but telling commentary on the power of the new technologies of the period to fascinate and to mystify. A spirit-writing typewriter is also featured in another lighthearted novel from the period, John Kendrick Bangs's *The Enchanted Type-Writer* (1899). The typewriter of the title is an old, disused machine that the story's narrator resurrects from the attic. This machine produces gibberish when the narrator attempts to type on it, but soon begins a career of automatic writing, producing pages of typescript "between the hours of midnight and four o'clock in the morning, . . . manipulated by unseen hands"(1). The spectral authors of this writing are the inhabitants of Hades, who produce, among other things, the *Stygian Gazette* (editor Jim Boswell) on the enchanted typewriter. The general tenor of these stories suggests that the social and cultural effects of relatively simple but new technologies could be profound and not as easy to understand or explain as the mechanics that drove them. Hence the curious incompatibility of the enchanted typewriter and the typing efforts of the narrator. The narrator is, however, male and his characterization of the manner in which his machine types its spectral messages is suggestive; it clicks along, he comments, as "merrily and as rapidly . . . as though some expert young woman were in charge" (10-11).

Behind the keys of their typewriters at least, fictional typewriter girls from the period are "in charge." Their specialized knowledge, because it is not well understood by most people, gives them a level of power over others. Accordingly, Bella is able to thwart her employer, Neal Larrard, in his efforts to dupe the gullible Pashleys with fake typewritten spirit-writing ("The Spirit of Sarah Keech"). In the "Swingley Green" episode, she is able to communicate clandestinely with Vincent Kendale, even under Larrard's watchful eye, via her typewriter. Her knowledge of the mechanical construction of the typewriter is also vital to Larrard's nefarious plans. Percy Whittaker, one of Larrard's confederates in crime, poses as a rich and indolent young man who hires Bella in order to watch her "tap [letters] out on that wonderful typewriter" (50), and incidentally to learn something about its mechanism; Bella obligingly instructs him in the mechanical operation and construction of her typewriter, knowledge for which Whittaker has unexpected uses. In order to carry out their dishonest plans, men who otherwise have knowledge and power that make Bella subordinate to them nevertheless must rely on her expertise at the typewriter, whether to help execute a fraud, as in "The Spirit of Sarah Keech" episode, or to maintain the appearance of the Secretarial Supply Syndicate as an efficient and legitimate business.

The importance of a business-like approach to her work becomes part of Bella's identity as "the girl behind the keys," an identification that both suggests impersonality and conflates the "girl" and her business function—the operation of the keys. The term most commonly used for a typist at this period of time—typewriter—makes an even more direct identification among the person, the role, and the machine. In a conversation with Larrard, for example, Daniel Maggs refers to Bella as "that typewriter of yours" (175). Bella herself acknowledges her role as impersonal employee. "[A] typist in my position has to become a mere machine," she admits; "her fingers are the only things that really matter about her" (34). Later, when working under duress with the clear knowledge that she is abetting crime, however unwillingly, she further withdraws into the mechanistic role and "work[s] like a machine" (144) or types "mechanically" (180).

While such a strong association of person and machine obviously has the potential to be dehumanizing, its force at the turn of the last century was quite otherwise. The introduction of the typewriter initially had a liberating effect on middle-class women because it provided an area of occupation and expertise that was both respectable and unassociated with traditional feminine roles. Typing, in other words, offered an option other than nursing, teaching, or indeed marriage. Juliet, the protagonist of another comic novel, Grant Allen's *The Type-Writer Girl* (1897), encapsulates the attitude of the period in her active rejection of a career as a teacher for one as a typist. "I should hate teaching," she says; "I prefer freedom" (79). Kate, the protagonist of *The Twelve-Pound Look*, a short play by J.M. Barrie, is even more assertive in her allegiance to technology. She leaves her "suffocatingly" successful husband for her typewriter, which, at the cost of twelve pounds, has provided the means for her independence. With the ability to earn her own living, Kate need no longer be subservient, even to a man who is "worth a quarter of million" (731). To be a typewriter was at least to be a free agent.

As such a free agent successfully negotiating the modern urban landscape and its distinctive social and commercial relations, Bella manifests the general characteristics of the New Woman. She is self-sufficient, both personally and financially, and independent in her thoughts and actions. Her interests and her career are non-traditional for her day. She seems completely at home in the business world, matching wits with shrewd and corrupt men. Domesticity does not seem to figure in her life or her character and she never lets feminine reserve get in the way of investigating the suspicious dealings of her employer and his confederates. On the face of things, then, Bella seems to be not just a New Woman, but a radical version of the New Woman, one prepared to encounter the seamiest side of human nature and human interaction. She confronts the modern world with a boldness not seen again until the advent of the worldly women who inhabit the realm of the hard-boiled detective in the works of American writers such as Dashiell Hammett and Raymond Chandler. Indeed, Bella anticipates, in her coupling of professional efficiency with almost uncanny instincts for sniffing out mysteries, the girl-Friday whose assistance is vital to the success of the male investigator in many early-to mid-twentieth-century detective stories, both in print and film media. But Bella, like the story she tells, also remains an odd hybrid of the new and the old, the modern and the Victorian. She frequently refers to herself in conventional terms of Victorian femininity as "only a weak woman" (110) or as "a weak girl" (144), or as responding to her "woman's wit" (58) or her "womanly curiosity" (130).

Virtually all Bella's actions belie these self-characterizations, however. She initially addresses her prospective employer at the Secretarial Supply Syndicate with "what boldness [she] could summon" (30), which, in the ensuing adventures, turns out to be considerable. She never accepts the dubious claims of her employer at face value but, while feigning ignorance or innocence, persists in uncovering his real intentions and in undermining his plans. While she does try at one point to resign from her position and the dangers inherent in it, confiding to her friend (and later fiancé) Phil that "the fight is too much for [her]" (110), she also admits that she had hoped he "might have put fresh courage into . . . [her], and urged . . . [her] to go on" (110). Moreover, when Larrard secures her continuance by means of virtual blackmail, she acquiesces and, while claiming to proceed with fear and trembling, continues her efforts to uncover and thwart his criminal intentions under cover of the completely inapposite persona he and his confederates have assigned to her—"the Lamb."

The cultural mix of the new and the old—of the technical or scientific and the mystical—that clusters around the idea of the typewriter in *The Girl Behind the Keys* is integrated into other parts of the story as well. "The Mummy" episode is the most obvious example of the combination of new science or scholarship with putative ancient wisdom. Throughout the nineteenth century, both professional and amateur scholars had been intensely interested in ancient civilizations and in uncovering knowledge and artefacts at archaeological digs. Popular fascination with Egyptian mummies and ancient curses, the Amra Ka incident reveals, had existed long before the opening of Tutankhamen's tomb in 1922. The Amra Ka episode is also curiously linked to "The Haunted Yacht," in that both assume the relative ease of travel to foreign countries and the permeability of borders, circumstances that produce potential perils as well as opportunities. Ancient sites can be plundered with impunity, their treasures transported to London under the cloak of scientific endeavour; Larrard can transport Bella and Arthur Crane (the engraver he is forcing to forge bank-notes) in a yacht, where they are out of the reach of any law enforcement agency; Bella in turn can set the yacht on fire, freeing herself and all other innocent parties, with no apparent fear of interference from the authorities in the Spanish town where they have docked. The world is thus expanding in alarming ways for Bella, as it was for many people who saw in the new century, in the emerging modern world, much promise and many hazards. With new ways of doing business, new ways of perceiving the world, and new knowledge comes the potential for misusing knowledge, and for duping the naïve and the unsuspecting. Opportunities were expanding for the confidence trickster as well as for the new professional or the technical expert.

The themes of intrigue and suspicion that run through *The Girl Behind the Keys*, as well as through other stories that feature technology in the late-Victorian and Edwardian era, reflect the undercurrent of alarm over—and even fear of—new knowledge and new technologies that was part of that culture, just as it is part of our culture today. The fear of the misuse or misappropriation of new knowledge, the fear of technology being used to dupe or to cheat, the fear above all of disorienting and unmanageable alterations in the social and cultural matrix—all these fears are simmering just beneath the comic surface. In other words, the defining symptoms of technology-paranoia characteristic of modern cultures are already evident in late-Victorian and Edwardian popular literature. The high-tech cheats in these stories are the precursors of the computer maniacs and hackers who turn up a century later in *Jurassic Park* and in episodes of *Law and Order*. The main source of reassurance, then as now, is that the same technology that can be a weapon in the hands of the deceitful and the corrupt can also be turned against them to foil their nefarious plans. The girl behind the keys is thus the prototype of the fictional computer whiz-kid who hacks the corrupt hacker and saves whatever is threatened—an individual, a community, a business, civilization as we know it—from doom.

PLACE AND MONETARY REFERENCES IN
THE GIRL BEHIND THE KEYS

Place references in *The Girl Behind the Keys* carry cultural significance that is sometimes lost on modern readers, especially on those who are unfamiliar with London and its suburbs. The reference to the "wilds of Tooting" on the opening page, for example, sets the tone for a novel that draws on the familiar and lightheartedly mocks it. Tooting, originally a quiet rural village, expanded during the suburban building boom at the turn of the century. It was hardly wild, in any sense of the word, but was considered relatively inaccessible until tram lines were extended there in the early twentieth century. Gallon uses specific street names (Tottenham Court Road, Oxford Street, the Strand), landmarks (Trafalgar Square, Marble Arch), areas within London (Covent Garden, Westminster), and suburbs (Tooting, Fulham) to construct a familiar, even mundane setting that he then plays off against the exotic and romantic—Egypt, the unnamed port in Spain where the *Mystic* drops anchor, and the fictitious Ancorania.

Monetary references are also unfamiliar to many modern

readers, even in England, as they are based on a system of pounds, shillings, and pence that was replaced in 1971 by the current decimal system. Until then, the breakdown was as follows:

One pound = twenty shillings (the gold pound coin was called a sovereign)
One shilling = twelve pence
One crown = five shillings
Half crown = two shillings and sixpence.

At the turn of the century, an income of about one pound a week was not uncommon for unskilled labourers and low-level office workers. This level of income would support a single person respectably and would support a small family at the poverty line. Women typically earned less than men doing the same or very similar work. When Bella considers asking for a weekly wage of thirty shillings (i.e. one pound and ten shillings), she is setting her sights high. The salary she is offered—three pounds per week—is unrealistically high, which is why she is elated and why the reader should immediately be suspicious of the Secretarial Supply Syndicate.

TOM GALLON

Tom Gallon was born in 1866 and as a very young man worked first as an office clerk and then as an usher in a large private school. He subsequently became secretary to the mayor of a provincial town. He began to write short stories about 1895, after illness had forced him to give up his clerical career. Gallon went on to write over forty novels, six plays, and numerous music hall sketches. His novels are peopled by ordinary but spirited characters, often from the working or lower middle classes. His works tend to be sensational, sentimental, or comic—sometimes, as in *The Girl Behind the Keys*, all at the same time—and several of his novels are mysteries. His most popular work was *Tatterley: The Story of a Dead Man* (1897), a highly sentimental novel with close parallels to Charles Dickens's *A Christmas Carol* in its plot and message.

WORKS CITED

Bangs, John Kendrick. *The Enchanted Type-Writer*. London and New York: Harper, 1899.

Barrie, J.M. "The Twelve-Pound Look." *The Plays of J.M. Barrie*. London: Hodder & Stoughton, 1929.

Marvin, Carolyn. *When Old Technologies Were New*. Oxford and New York: Oxford UP, 1988.

Parry, E.A. "Mr. Twistleton's Type-Writer." *Cornhill Magazine* 54 (1887): 62-71.

Raynor, Olive Pratt [Grant Allen]. *The Type-Writer Girl*. London: Pearson, 1897. Rpt. Ed. Clarissa J. Suranyi. Peterborough, ON: Broadview Press, 2004.

Zimmeck, Meta. "Jobs for the Girls: The Expansion of Clerical Work for Women, 1850-1914." *Unequal Opportunities: Women's Employment in England 1800-1918*. Ed. Angela V. John. Oxford: Blackwell, 1986. 153-77.

SUGGESTIONS FOR FURTHER READING

Cadogan, Mary and Patricia Craig. *The Lady Investigates: Women Detectives and Spies in Fiction*. New York: St. Martin's Press, 1981.

Keep, Christopher. "The Cultural Work of the Type-Writer Girl." *Victorian Studies* 40:3 (Spring 1997): 401-26.

Klein, Kathleen Gregory. *The Woman Detective: Gender and Genre*. Chicago and Urbana: University of Illinois Press, 1988.

Knight, Stephen. *Form and Ideology in Crime Fiction*. Bloomington: Indiana UP, 1980.

Ledger, Sally. *The New Woman Reader: Fiction and Feminism at the fin de siècle*. Manchester and New York: Manchester UP, 1997.

Nelson, Carolyn Christensen, ed. *A New Woman Reader: Fiction, Articles, and Drama of the 1890s*. Peterborough, ON: Broadview Press, 2001.

Price, Leah and Pamela Thurschwell, eds. *Literary Secretaries/ Secretarial Culture*. Aldershot: Ashgate, 2005

Thomas, Ronald R. *Detective Fiction and the Rise of Forensic Science*. Cambridge and New York: Cambridge UP, 1999.

Thurschwell, Pamela. *Literature, Technology and Magical Thinking, 1880-1920*. Cambridge: Cambridge UP, 2001.

Young, Arlene. "Bachelor Girls and Working Women." *Culture, Class and Gender in the Victorian Novel: Gentlemen, Gents and Working Women*. Houndmills: Macmillan, 1999. 119-56.

A Note on the Text

The text is based on the original 1903 edition of the novel (London: Hutchinson) and is unchanged except for the addition of a few missing punctuation marks and the correction of obvious typographical errors.

THE GIRL BEHIND THE KEYS

THE KIDNAPPING OF PRESIDENT PENALUNA.

I was down to the last sixpence—and I was a woman. Put yourself in my place, in the great and brutal world of London, with sixpence standing between you and starvation.[1] Put it that you had not tasted food since noon of the previous day, and that it was then four o'clock in the evening of the day following. Add to that, that you had not a single friend in London (save one, to whom it was impossible to appeal, because he was as poor as I was), and you will get some faint idea of what I felt like.

One-and-twenty—and facing the world with sixpence! This was the end of things; I had had a hard and bitter struggle, and there was nothing else to be done. And I was very cold, and very tired, and remarkably miserable.

I had one small room, at the top of a dreary old house, in a small turning off the Tottenham Court Road. I have walked past it many times since, and smiled to think of that afternoon; but it was no smiling matter then. I had that curious lump in my throat, and that pain at the back of my neck, which told me that despair had me in its grip, and that there was no hope anywhere.

I wondered what was best to be done; I had a mad thought of going to appeal to my landlady for some food—no matter of what kind—that should keep life in me for a few hours. Of course,

---

[1] See the section on place and monetary references in the "Introduction" (18-19).

that was out of the question; I owed money for rent already, and I had to keep my desperate need hidden. Feeling chilled, as well as hungry, I started to light the fire in the small grate.

The paper which had been thrust in at the bottom of the grate burnt out, and smouldered away, and refused to light the wood above it. Despairingly, I looked round for something else; and saw the morning newspaper, folded up as it had been brought to me. I tore a sheet from it, and proceeded to light the fire again. It happened that, quite early that morning, I had gone out to the wilds of Tooting, to try and secure a place as a governess; that excursion had swallowed up my day, and the last of my money (save the sixpence), and I had had no time to look at the paper. Now, as I watched the flame stealing along it, I am afraid a tear or two gathered in my eyes, at the thought of the melancholy fate before me.

Even that piece of paper wouldn't light; part of it burnt out, and the rest dropped into the fender. Determined to try no more, I picked it up, and glanced at it, idly enough. Just where the scorched edge came, I read these words:—

"Secretarial Supply Syndicate, Limited.—Young lady required, with knowledge of typewriting. Must possess great tact, and be willing to travel, if necessary. Good salary. —Address, Manager—"

Here followed the address—in a building overlooking Trafalgar Square. Perhaps I am a little superstitious; at all events, it seemed as though this offer had been flung to me, like this, at the last moment. I thought no more of the fire; I forgot that I was cold and hungry; I put on my hat and coat again, and started for Trafalgar Square. As I left the house, I looked a little ruefully at my shabby clothes, and began to doubt whether or not I should stand any real chance.

I reached the place, and climbed a dark stair. Various names were painted on the upper ground-glass portions of various doors—names of utterly unknown Companies, which, I thought, in all probability, were never meant to pay dividends. At last I came to a door on which was painted the title for which I was looking—"The Secretarial Supply Syndicate, Limited." The paint was very new—so new, that I could see the lines marked on the glass which had guided the painter.

Just as I raised my hand to knock at the door, it was opened, and a man stood in the doorway. He was so large a man, that he filled the doorway completely, or so it seemed to me at that time; and I, being small of stature, and by no means robust, quailed a little before him. Remembering that sixpence in my pocket, I spoke, however, with more boldness than I felt.

"If you please—are you the manager?"

"Yes—I am the manager," said the big man, and stepped back into the room. "Pray come in."

I went into the room; and noted, first of all, that it was very well furnished. Like the painting on the door, however, the furniture was new; one might almost have said that the varnish upon it was scarcely dry. The big man removed his hat, and placed it on a desk; then waved a white hand towards a chair. I sat down.

"And what may I have the pleasure of doing for you, Madam?" he asked.

Looking at him in the fading light of the afternoon, I saw that he was exceedingly good-looking, and very well dressed. He had a large head, closely covered with thick brown, curling hair; the nose was long and straight; the eyes just a trifle too near together, perhaps; the mouth a mere strong straight line. Not a bad face, take it for all in all.

With what boldness I could summon, I stated my errand; he nodded from time to time, while I told him what my qualifications were, and what I could do. Finally, without a word, he got up from the desk, and went across to a table in the corner of the room, on which stood a typewriter under its case. Lifting the case off, with something of a flourish and a clatter, he signed to me to take my seat at the table.

"Write what I say," he said, quietly.

I quickly pushed a sheet of paper into the machine, and sat ready. He only dictated one sentence to me, but about as rapidly as I've ever heard a man speak.

"If the man who travels unknown and alone comes to-night, he does not leave the place alive. Remember the terms of the ransom."

That was a little bit startling; but you get used to things in this world. Incidentally, I may say that I once typed a novel for a madman, who began in the Garden of Eden, and finished at the Marble Arch. In this particular case, I simply took down the words as an exercise in speed and accuracy; then folded my hands in my lap, and waited for the next. To my surprise, the big man laughed, and dropped one white firm hand on my shoulder.

"You'll do," he said, in a low voice. "Give me the paper."

I took it out of the machine, and handed it to him; he tore it into a dozen pieces, and dropped them on to the last glowing embers in the office fire.

"I like to see anyone of your stamp," he said, looking at me coolly. "When can you begin work?"

"At once," I said, almost breaking down then, at this sudden good fortune, and wondering dimly if I might ask for thirty shillings a week.

"Good. Any friends in London?"

I thought of the one friend; but he didn't concern anyone else; so I said quickly—"No—not one."

"Good," said the man again. "Come to-morrow at eleven; I'll give you three pounds a week."

I am not emotional—but I nearly hugged him. Three pounds a week!—and I had been down to my last sixpence! When I recovered myself, the man was speaking.

"You have only to remember one thing, if you work here," he said. "We have a very high-class typewriting office, and we deal only with special clients. Discretion is necessary; that is to say, if a secretary is sent out to one of these clients, she must forget, at the end of a day, all that has happened during that day. You understand?"

"Certainly," I said. "I understand perfectly."

"I thought you would," he said, with a curious smile." I am not often mistaken in people; I don't think I shall be mistaken in you. It has been my fate to interview some sixty odd members of your sex to-day; you are the one woman for my purpose."

I did not then understand what he meant; I did not know the part I had to play in the business with which he was connected. All that I knew was that, by great good luck, I happened to suit the taste of this new employer, and that he was prepared to pay me a much larger salary than I had hoped to receive. Elated with my success, I was going out of the door, after bidding him a formal "Good-night," when he called me back again.

"You quite understand that it may be necessary for you to be sent to any part of the country—I was almost going to say, to any part of the world—at a moment's notice?" he asked.

"It is a matter of indifference to me," I replied.

"You're an independent young woman," he retorted, with a smile. "By the way, I want to be sure of securing you in the morning; shall we say that your—your salary is paid in advance?"

I lied heroically, and again said that was a matter of perfect indifference to me.

"I prefer to pay in advance," he said, dipping his hand into his pocket—"one never knows what may happen."

Behold me, then, walking out of the office of The Secretarial Supply Syndicate, Limited, with three pounds and sixpence in my pocket, and the knowledge that I was in possession of an income. It did not matter to me how long that income was to last; for the moment, my troubles were at an end.

I dined well that night, and slept better; in the morning, having made some little cheap additions to my toilet, I arrived at the office of the Syndicate considerably before eleven o'clock. The manager whom I had seen on the previous day was not there; in charge of the place I found a smart, alert-looking boy, who eyed me up and down, and seemed altogether somewhat suspicious of me. I explained who I was; and he requested me to take a chair, and wait for "the guv'nor."

He gave himself airs, that boy; he was obviously, in his own mind, the boy who knew all about the business, whilst I was a hopeless outsider. Presently he looked up, and addressed me.

"Not a bad little lunch party we shall 'ave 'ere, Miss," he

said, condescendingly. "If you take my tip, don't stand no lip from the guv'nor."

"I won't," I said, striving to hide a smile.

"That's right, Miss. W'en you've bin in the business as long as I 'ave, you'll understand that there's things goes on in this office as'd curl the 'air on a door knob. What we don't know an' don't do, ain't worth knowin' an' doin'—an' wot we—"

There was a telephone fixed up against the wall; and at that moment it rang. Now the boy was small, and it was quite impossible for him to reach it, unless he dragged a chair across for the purpose. Before he could do so, I had the telephone at my ear, and was speaking sharply into it.

"Hullo! Who are you?"

"Grimes," came the reply, in a muffled voice. "Are you Syndicate?"

"Yes," I said. "What is it."

"Mr. Penton—without his moustache—arrives this morning at twelve. Can the Secretary meet him?"

"Of course," I replied, feeling that I was responsible for things.

"All right. You know the time and place," came the voice again. "Good-bye!"

I heard the mysterious Grimes "ring off"; I "rang off" also, and came back to my chair.[1]

"Wot's it all about?" asked the boy.

"Haven't the least idea," I replied; and at that moment the manager came in. He bowed very politely to me, and nodded curtly to the boy. He passed into an inner room; and, after a

---

[1]   Telephone connections were terminated by signalling a central switchboard ("ringing off"), usually by means of a hand crank on the side of the transmitter box.

moment or two, called me in. I went in, and closed the door behind me.

As he motioned me to a chair, he suddenly got up, and strode across the office and called to the boy outside. "Any message this morning?" he asked.

"The young lady took a message from the telephone," replied the boy.

The man closed the door, and came back again. "You've begun early," he said, with a smile. "What was the message?"

I repeated it to him, and he nodded over each word. When I had finished, he looked up at me.

"That doesn't seem to surprise you," he remarked; and I saw that curious smile flicker over his face again.

"Why should it?" I asked. "You seem to forget that a typist in my position has to become a mere machine; her fingers are the only things that really matter about her."

"That's right," he replied. "That's just what I want you to think. You may have to do some curious things; I want you to do them, keeping always that calm impassive look on your innocent face, and saying nothing about them. Now, this message this morning is for you."

"One of your clients?" I asked; and he nodded. "By-the-way," I added—"I ought to know the name of my employer."

"Your employer is the Syndicate," he replied; "but I might as well tell you my name. It is Larrard—Neal Larrard."

"Well, Mr. Neal Larrard—what instructions have you for me to-day?" I asked.

"You will pack up the machine, and will go straight to the address I have written on this paper," replied the big man. "There you are engaged by the day, as secretary to Mr. Penton—"

"Without the moustache?" I asked, quietly.

"Miss Thorn," he said, in a hard voice—"you will find it well not to remember too much sometimes. At this address you will type such letters as you may be requested to do, and will place yourself generally at the disposal of Mr. Penton. I would urge you to remember, Miss Thorn, that we are paying you a large salary, and that we expect a good return for it. Come to the office to-night—at whatever time it may be—when your duties are ended. You will find me here. Remember also that (I do not speak in any unkind or discourteous sense) you become the servant of whoever employs you from this office."

Remembering that three pounds I had received on the previous evening, and how it had saved me from possible starvation, I humbly said that I understood. By the direction of Mr. Larrard, in five minutes more I was speeding away in a cab,[1] with the typewriter on the seat beside me, in the direction of a certain quiet little hotel in South Kensington.

I entered the hotel, the porter following with my typewriter. The directions on the written paper I held were that I was to ask for Mr. Grimes. Following those instructions, I was shown into a room which seemed to be a species of small coffee-room, and which was empty. A moment later, the door was opened, and a tall thin-faced man glided in, and closed the door behind him. He was dressed in very respectable black; and might have been anything—from an undertaker to a chapel-keeper. He came towards me, and spoke my name.

"Miss Bella Thorn?"

I acknowledged it; and the man solemnly handed me a chair.

---

[1] I.e. a hansom cab, a two-wheeled, horse-drawn vehicle.

I began to wonder when Mr. Penton (without his moustache) would appear.

"Now, Miss Thorn," he began, in a business-like tone—"you will understand that I am the agent for the Syndicate of which Mr. Neal Larrard is manager. In a word, I introduce clients. Before I introduce *you* to this particular client, Mr. Penton, I would like to make a few suggestions. Are you listening?"

"Very carefully, Mr. Grimes," I replied.

"This Mr. Penton is somewhat eccentric, and highly nervous; he is in this country on a semi-political mission; he may have business letters to dictate to you. On the other hand, he may have letters of another character to dictate to you—letters to a lady. You will understand that Mr. Penton, by an unfortunate accident in travelling, has broken his right arm, so that it is impossible for him to write; hence the need for your services. Having made this explanation, I will introduce you to him."

He took up the typewriter in its case, and walked with it out of the room; I followed. A moment or two later I found myself bowing to a polite and dapper little gentleman, with his arm in a black sling, and with a good-tempered clean-shaven face. Within five minutes, Mr. Grimes had disappeared, and I sat down at a table before my machine, ready to commence work.

It was the queerest work I had ever done. The little man sat lounging in a chair, smoking cigarettes, and dictating to me, in a high-pitched voice, and with a decidedly foreign accent, various little letters and notes—most of which were to personal friends. At last there came one letter, which was not exactly to a personal friend, but which was a decidedly embarrassing letter for a young typist to write.

It was a love letter. Apparently taking not the faintest notice of my presence, he began to pour out, in most ardent tones, the most ardent phrases; compared the lady to nearly every planet he could think of, except the warlike one; and begged that she would see him, after having brought him so many thousand miles in her train. When he had finished the letter, and I had taken it from the machine, he addressed me.

"I have been told that you will act for me as—how shall I put it?—as a messenger, if it be necessary. The sweet lady to whom I have written sends to me from an address in London here; will you convey to her the message that is on this paper, and bring back her answer. One of your cabs will take you, and can bring you back again. These other letters also you will be good enough to put into the post box."

I sealed up the letter, and addressed it; but, before that, I had held it firmly on the table, while, with his left hand, the man scrawled a name upon it. Glancing at it, as he wrote the name, I saw that it was not Penton, although it began with a "Pen—" and then ended in a scrawl. I stamped the other letters, and went out to find a cab.

To my infinite surprise, Mr. Grimes suddenly appeared from nowhere—or so it seemed—with a cab waiting. Without a word, he assisted me in, and we drove off. Evidently he knew the address to which I was going; for, when I turned to him, and began to speak, he raised his hand, and informed me coolly that he knew all about it, and that we were going to the right place. The address was in Fulham—not a very great distance from the hotel in which Mr. Penton was staying; which probably accounted for his presence in that neighbourhood.

The house to which we drove was a boarding-house of a rather squalid type. Mr. Grimes, getting out with me, led me into the place and up some stairs. In a room on the first floor I confronted the lady to whom that passionate letter had been addressed. She was a tall, dark-eyed woman, exceedingly handsome, and far better dressed than I should have anticipated, considering the place in which I found her.

She took not the faintest notice of me; with Mr. Grimes standing watching, she read the letter through contemptuously; and then, to my astonishment, handed it to him. He read it impassively, and then spoke to her. I have omitted to mention, by the way, that the envelope of the letter bore the name of Madame Jevaux.

"You will answer it, of course," said Grimes, while I stood looking at them in bewilderment.

"What else am I here for?" she retorted; and swept across the room to a writing table, and sat down there. She wrote at a great rate, and only a line or two; then she handed a sealed letter to me.

"You will take this back to Mr.—Mr. Penton, and deliver it immediately," she said. "See that you deliver it to the gentleman—and to him only."

Wondering more than ever, I left Mr. Grimes there, and came away. Back to the hotel again, as fast as the cab would take me; Mr. Penton received me with the greatest impatience—tore open the letter, and read the contents. I saw him put his delicate fingers to his lips, and blow a kiss into the air; then he thrust the letter into his pocket, and prepared to go.

"I need not detain you any longer," he said to me. "My mission is accomplished, and your work is done. You have done admirably, my little one; good-day to you!"

I saw him run out of the room, in a great state of excitement; and knew that he was making straight for that woman in the boarding-house in Fulham. However, it didn't concern me; I leisurely packed up my machine, and went downstairs, intending to tell a porter to fetch the machine for me, and to put it in a cab.

Then a surprising thing occurred. At the bottom of the stairs I encountered that one friend to whom I have referred—Mr. Philip Esdaile. I had been so completely astonished that day, that there was no room in me for further surprise; indeed, it seemed the most natural thing in the world to see Philip there. Perhaps I ought to say, in this place, that Philip Esdaile had had certain wild ideas concerning me, and had been anxious that I should become Mrs. Esdaile; as he was a young and struggling journalist, I scarcely thought it would be a wise step; so, with a little mutual misunderstanding, we had parted; and now here he was again.

He beckoned me into the empty coffee-room; I followed, expecting a scene. But his first words were startling.

"Well—where have you sent that man?"

While I was staring at him in perplexity, he caught me by the arms, and began to speak rapidly.

"I had no idea, till I saw you come here this morning, that you were in the business," he said; "I've been on the track of it for months; it's the biggest thing I've ever had yet for copy. It's a gigantic conspiracy; this man who calls himself Penton is the victim of it. But how on earth are you concerned in it?"

I briefly explained to him the secretaryship I had been fortunate enough to secure; I gave him a rapid outline of the people I had met, and of my introduction to this Mr. Penton. He listened, with an elated face.

"This is absolutely splendid!" he exclaimed. "The gentleman who sent the love-letter, my dear Bella, is no other than a certain Penaluna, Perpetual President of the State of Ancorania—never mind where. Suffice it that this is a matter of kidnapping; and that this Madame Jevaux is the decoy used to take this man, and to hold him. Your precious Secretarial Supply Syndicate is nothing more nor less than the gang who have organised the whole business. And you have been innocently working for that gang."

Gradually, as Philip went on speaking eagerly, I began to see that he knew all about it; and had, as he had said, been on the track of it for months, for journalistic reasons. We discussed what was best to be done; and I gave him the address of that fourth-rate little boarding-house in Fulham.

"I'll go there at once," he said—"and, as you are mixed up with the gang, it might be well for you to mistake your instructions, and go there also. Your machine will be safe here, and can be sent for at any time."

So we started for Fulham again—Philip going his own way, and I engaging, at his suggestion, another cab, and driving off at top speed. When I got to the house, I walked quietly past the servant who admitted me, giving her a curt nod as I did so; having admitted me on the previous occasion, she made no attempt to stop me now; and I went up the stairs to the door of the room in which I had found Madame Jevaux.

As I reached the door, certain curious sounds could be heard from within the room. It seemed impossible, until I remembered what Philip had told me; but there almost appeared to be a desperate struggle in progress. Not very loud; but I heard the trampling of feet, and then the heavy fall of a body. Perhaps in that boarding-house they were used to disturbances; at all events, they took no notice of this one. After a moment or two, while I stood there hesitating, the door of the room was cautiously opened, and the face of Mr. Grimes—a little heated, I thought—looked out. Seeing me, he came out on to the landing, closing the door behind him.

"What do you want?" he asked, in a whisper, putting his face close to mine.

"Nothing," I replied, with the most innocent look I could assume at that short notice. "I thought I was to come back here."

"No—no; entirely a mistake," he said. "But now you are here, it may be well for you to remain a minute or two."

He went back into the room; and, a moment later, the door opened again, and Madame Jevaux sauntered out. She was laughing, and seemed in high spirits. Following her came a man—thick set and powerful-looking—with a face of the most villainous type I ever remember to have seen. Grimes came last; he locked the door on the outside, and handed me the key.

"Straight back to the office," he said; "and deliver this into the hands of Mr. Larrard; give it to no one else."

Events followed so rapidly after that, that I have only a confused notion of what really happened. I remember that the three of them went downstairs rather hurriedly, leaving me alone there; I remember that, as I turned to go myself down the darkened stairway, someone seemed to shoot out from another room; a hand was laid over my mouth, and the key wrested from my grasp. It was Philip Esdaile.

"It's all right," he breathed— "I've got the whole copy out— only had to add a note or two, after what you told me—and it's gone down to the *Evening Wire*[1] by special messenger. Now for the last act."

"What are you going to do?" I asked.

"Simply let myself into this room, and give you the key again. You will then lock it on the outside, and take it to this man Larrard, as you have been instructed to do. Don't hesitate; there's no danger; as a journalist, I merely require a private interview with Mr. Penaluna, Perpetual President of Ancorania; and I don't wish to be interrupted."

It was very hard work, locking that door on Philip; but I had to do it. I felt utterly wretched and frightened; for Phil is a good sort, and he's about the only friend I possess. However, I believed in him; so I locked the door, after letting him into the room, and carried the key with me down the stairs; then I drove to the office of the Syndicate.

Mr. Neal Larrard was absolutely beaming. "It's the smartest thing—and the quickest—I ever remember in my life," he said, rubbing his hands. "As for you, Miss Thorn—you're a treasure; you're cheap at your price. Now I'll go down, and see our man."

"Might I come too?" I asked, literally shaking from head to foot, but yet striving to preserve some of that stolid impassiveness which was my most valuable stock-in-trade.

He looked at me in astonishment. "You? What for?"

"I—I should like to see the fun," I said, meekly.

"By Jove!—so you shall," he said, looking at me whimsically. "One doesn't often meet a girl like you; you'll go far, young woman!"

---

[1]   A fictitious newspaper.

We drove down together. Mr. Neal Larrard was evidently well known at the boarding-house; he was admitted without question. Quite triumphantly, and with an easy assurance about him, he went up the stairs, and put the key in the lock of the door. At the last moment, he turned, and whispered to me—"I've never seen the man; only heard his description. I believe he has a scar across one side of his forehead. Is that so?"

I had noticed that mark on Mr. Penton, and I said that it was so. Mr. Neal Larrard nodded, unlocked the door, and went in.

In the semi-darkened room, we saw a figure seated at a table, with its head buried on its arms. Mr. Larrard carefully locked the door, and then spoke, in some excitement:

"Why—they told me they had bound him securely. What on earth—?"

He went swiftly up to the table, and dropped a hand on the shoulder of the figure; the man raised his head, and disclosed the face of Philip Esdaile. I almost cried out, because I had not known him in that half-darkened room.

"Mr. Neal Larrard," said Philip—"you have the wrong pig by the ear. President Penaluna is gone; the game is up!"

"Why—who are you?" cried Larrard; and I saw his hand move towards the breast pocket of his coat.

"Oh—don't do anything rash, Mr. Larrard," said Philip, quietly. "I lighted on the matter by accident; I have spied upon you for a long time. I knew that Madame Jevaux was your decoy; I knew that she had lured this man over to England, and was gradually bringing him into your hands. I believe he had an unfortunate accident, a little time ago—a carriage accident—and broke his arm; you would have been better pleased, perhaps, had he not escaped your clutches then. May I suggest that the carriage accident was arranged?"

"Suggest what you like," said Larrard, grimly. "Go on."

"You failed to get him into your hands after the carriage accident—arranged by your men; then you tried this business direct. He was to be brought here; bound and gagged; held to ransom. It was to be put about that he was on a not very creditable errand; the threat of exposure was to be made; he was to be set free only after payment of a large sum."

"Where is he now?" asked Larrard. "Or have those fools taken the wrong man?"

"They got the right man once; but President Penaluna went out of that window behind me, and so got away, some ten minutes ago. I assisted him; but thought it better to remain, in order to explain his absence."

"How did you get into this room?" asked Larrard.

"There is always the window," said Philip, with a quick look at me.

"Very well, my friend; you have made a mistake, in setting me at defiance. You shall take the place of the President, my young friend; you are in our hands, and we will do what we like with you. Miss Thorn"—he turned to me quickly —"you may go."

"Stop—there is no necessity for that," said Philip, coolly. "At the office of the *Evening Wire*, there rests, at this moment, a full and complete account, Mr. Larrard, of this conspiracy. The story has been known to me for some time; I got the details—the final details—only to-day. Unless I return to the office by four o'clock, that report, with the necessary headlines, goes into type, and floods London to-night with the sensational story of the kidnapping of President Penaluna. On the other hand, if I walk out of this place quietly and unmolested, I return to the office of the *Evening Wire*, and"—Philip glanced again at me for a moment—"I destroy the article. President Penaluna is gone—and there is an end of the matter."

There was an end of the matter; Philip Esdaile walked out of the room, smiling quietly to himself; and Mr. Larrard went back—a beaten man—to the office of the Syndicate. He did not suspect me; indeed, there was no reason why he should. It was only Philip (I saw him that evening for five minutes) who rejoiced over the ending, for my sake.

"He never guessed about you," said Phil. "But—oh, my dear Bella—what a beautiful bit of journalism thrown away!"

"And my situation thrown away, too," I said, bitterly.

"My dear girl—not a bit of it!" he cried. "Have you pluck enough to go on; to fight these people in the dark; to bring a dangerous gang, perhaps, to justice?"

"I'll try," I said, faintly. "But I'm only a weak woman, Phil."

"And in your weakness and your simplicity, Bella, shall be your strength," he said, laughing. "Begin again to-morrow, with a stout heart. All will be well."

I inwardly hoped all would be well, and went home to my little room with a doubting heart.

THE DIAMONDS OF THE DANSEUSE.

I own that it was with very mixed feelings that I went back, the next morning, to the office of the "Secretarial Supply Syndicate, Limited." After that affair concerning President Penaluna, I scarcely knew what would happen, or how I might be received. But for my promise to Mr. Philip Esdaile, I do not think I could have faced the business any longer; there was, however, yet another reason. I had been paid for a week in advance; and, quite apart from the fact that that money—or some part of it—had already been spent for necessities of living, I, being an honest little person, felt that I had yet to earn it. After all, they could not suspect me as having had anything to do with that unfortunate matter of the escape of the President. So I went back, though somewhat tremblingly.

For a couple of days nothing happened. If I had needed any confirmation of the kind of place I was in, I received it then, during those days, in the fact that I had nothing to do. The manager—Mr. Neal Larrard—put in an appearance on the first day; and was for a long time alone in his office; presently he put his head out, and called to me.

"Miss Thorn—one moment, please."

I went in. He was standing with his back to the fireplace, and he nodded to me curtly to shut the door. I did so, and never took my eyes off him from that moment.

"Well—have you anything to say to me?" he asked. "Anything about our friend the President, for instance?"

I shook my head slowly, and looked at him in apparent surprise. "I don't understand," I said.

"Neither do I," he said, with a grin. "Either you are precious dangerous, or precious useful."

"I think you don't quite realise the position," I said, quietly. "I am, as I explained to you, Mr. Larrard, quite alone in London; and I have my living to earn. You have been good enough to engage me for certain typewriting duties, and to pay me a very liberal salary. If I perform those duties to your satisfaction—surely that is enough?"

"More than enough, Miss Thorn," he said, throwing back his head, and laughing silently up towards the ceiling. "You're a little wonder; I've never seen anyone quite like you in my life. 'Pon my word—I'm not sure that I won't give you a share."

"I am here at a salary which is more than sufficient for my wants," I said, holding up a protesting hand. "Let that suffice. I don't in the least understand what you mean—and I don't wish to. Have you any other instructions, Mr. Larrard?"

He shook his head, and I went out, leaving him still laughing, in that silent fashion, up at the ceiling. He went away an hour later, without a word.

For two days Bob Pilcher, the office boy, and I had the place to ourselves. I suppose that no one particularly wanted a typist at that time, at all events from the office of the Secretarial Supply Syndicate; whatever the reason, no one came. I kept my machine—or rather the office machine—in good order, and read a couple of novels. On the third day, the telephone rang violently, and I answered it.

"Is that you, Miss Thorn?" It was the voice of the manager, Mr. Neal Larrard.

"Yes, Mr. Larrard," I replied.

"Has anyone been; any—any business been doing?"

"Nothing whatever," I told him.

"I want you to take the machine, in a cab, at once to Leaver's Hotel, in Blade Street, Covent Garden. Ask for Mr. Percy Whittaker; he wants your services for the day. Are you sure you understand?"

I repeated the address to him, and I heard him say that it was all right. Inwardly wondering if it *was* all right, I packed up the machine, and started off on that few minutes' journey.

I was shewn up to the private sitting room of Mr. Percy Whittaker. Leaver's Hotel was ultra-respectable—one of those solid old-fashioned places, with an unimpeachable bald-headed head waiter, and a slow solemnity about it. On entering the sitting room, I saw Mr. Percy Whittaker yawning at a window; he turned quickly towards me, and restored my hopes in a moment. I felt that we were at last embarking on respectable business. He was so very elegant, and so very gentlemanly.

He was quite a young man, dressed in the very height of fashion; he had a single eyeglass stuck in one eye. He advanced towards me, with a courtesy that was the finest I had ever encountered, and apologised profusely for having given me so much trouble. I arranged my machine on a table in the window, and prepared for my duties.

Mr. Percy Whittaker told me, in an elegant drawl, that he was not sure, after all, whether he wanted me. "The truth of the matter is, my dear young lady," he said—"it's just a question of a new sensation. An idle man, I want to be more idle still; I hate writing letters, and I thought it wouldn't be half bad fun just to talk them, as it were, and see you tap them out on that wonderful typewriter. Let's try—shall we?"

He was more like a good-humoured boy than anything else; and he was wonderfully interested in the machine. He got me to explain all about it, and what the parts were for; and we wasted the whole morning, without a sentence being written. When I delicately reminded him of this, he airily told me that he did not mind in the least, and that he had enjoyed himself immensely. Just after he had suggested that I should go to lunch, he suddenly called to me, and begged to know what "those little round things, like barrels" were, at the ends of the machine. I explained to him again that they were the barrels on which the ribbon was wound; and I expended another quarter of an hour in unwinding the ribbon and showing him the little metal cylinder on which it automatically wound itself up.

He was very interested indeed; and got me to show him all the screws, and everything connected with it. "I know you'll excuse me," he said, with that delightful laugh of his—"but I'm like a child with a new toy. I shall really buy one of these things—just to play with, you know. I think I'd better take you out to lunch now—hadn't I?"

"I don't think that would be quite the proper sort of thing," I reminded him, demurely. "I am simply in your employ."

"Oh, I'm sorry, I'm sure," he said; "but I daresay you know best. In half an hour, then—or shall we say an hour?"

I said I thought half an hour would be sufficient; but he urged me not to hurry back on his account. The last thing I saw, as I went out of the room, was Mr. Percy Whittaker, still closely examining "those funny little round things" at the ends of the machine, and chuckling softly to himself, in boyish enjoyment.

It happened that I finished my lunch (always a very modest affair in those days) quite early, and came out into the streets again. Then, as ill luck would have it, it began to rain quite smartly; I could not go back again, and I scarcely knew what to do for the remaining half hour. Finally, I decided to go back to Leaver's Hotel, and to explain why I had cut that hour short.

Just as I was crossing the road towards the hotel, a shouting news-boy crossed in front of me, with his contents bill[1] fluttering in the wind, and with the chief item on it pumping breathlessly from his lips.

"Great Jewel Robbery on a Channel Steamer. Speshul!"

For no particular reason, I bought a paper; perhaps it occurred to me that I might have nothing to do, until Mr. Percy Whittaker returned from what would probably be a more elaborate lunch than mine, and might be glad to read. At the hotel, I found that they recognised me as that very harmless individual, a typist engaged for the day; the clerk handed me the key of Mr. Whittaker's private sitting room. At the same time he made a puzzling remark.

"If the lady should require anything, will you please ring?"

Before I had time to reply he had gone back into his little office. As I hesitated for a moment, it occurred to me that he might be referring to me; and that that extremely gentlemanly

---

[1] "Contents bills"—usually hand-written posters featuring the major, or sometimes just the most sensational, headline of the day—are still common features of London newsstands. In the late nineteenth and early twentieth centuries, news boys would call out the headlines as they stood on street corners or passed through the streets selling newspapers.

man, Mr. Percy Whittaker, might have left word that my wants were to be attended to. I went on up the stairs with the key—let myself in—and opened the paper.

That chief item only consisted of some seven or eight lines, with a huge heading. It seemed that a celebrated Continental danseuse—La Belle Obrino—travelling to England by the night boat, accompanied only by her maid, had left in charge of that maid her diamonds. Rumour whispered that one particular necklace had been presented to her by a certain Royal personage; that it was almost priceless; and that it had disappeared. The maid had made friends with a supposed gentleman's servant, travelling on the same boat; and that gentleman's servant had assisted her with the luggage. The gentleman's servant had unaccountably disappeared, and the diamonds of La Belle Obrino had disappeared with him. Active search was being made, but the police had no actual clue.

I really do not know why that particular case should have interested me so much; all I know is, that I read the brief description of that wonderful necklace over and over again, until I almost had the number of stones, and the very size of them by heart. Just as I was folding the paper to put it aside, a curious sound startled me, and I sprang to my feet.

I was alone in the room; yet that sound had seemed to be quite near me. Looking round quickly, I saw a door in one corner, with a key on my side of the lock. I went across to it cautiously, and listened. The sound came from the other side of that door.

It was a moaning noise—with certain words to fill in the pauses between the moaning. It was almost as though someone were talking in their sleep. While I listened, there came to me the remembrance of what the clerk of the hotel had said about the lady. For the voice on the other side of that door was that of a woman; and, curiously enough, I seemed to recognise it.

I suppose I had been excited by reading that sensational story in the paper; I suppose I was, at that time, on the alert for anything and everything that might happen. At all events, I know that I turned the key in the door, and, after one quick look round the room in which I stood, pulled open the door, and looked in. The sight I beheld was a startling one.

On a couch in that inner room lay the figure of a woman— moving restlessly, and muttering to herself. At sight of her, I gave a sort of cry, and ran forward into the room. For I knew her.

It was Madame Jevaux—that handsome creature who had been responsible for the capture of President Penaluna in my first adventure with the Syndicate. Although I was surprised to see her there, and although I instinctively felt that I was again plunged into the midst of some scheme with which she was connected, the circumstance of finding her there was not the strange part of the business at all. The strange part of it was that, as she lay there, apparently asleep, she wore upon her neck and bosom a glittering array of diamonds. Plainly dressed though she was, the things—fit to adorn a princess—were clasped about her neck, and lay upon the breast that was moved by her troubled breathing.

Yet a more curious thing still. The dress had been unfastened, and turned in at the neck and bosom, so that the stones rested upon the bare white flesh—as though she would feel the touch of them, even in her sleep.

I had nothing to guide me, of course; but, instinctively,

my thoughts darted back to that sensational bit of news in the paper I had bought. I could know nothing of the gang with which I was innocently connected, however much I might suspect; and it seemed to me possible that this woman, whom I already knew to have been connected with a shady business, and whom I now found locked away in a room in a quiet hotel, might be concerned in this great jewel robbery. While I stood there, wondering what I should do, I heard footsteps and voices on the stairs outside; on the impulse of the moment, I closed that communicating door, leaving myself in the inner room with the sleeping woman, and looked wildly round for a place in which to hide.

It would never do for me to be found in that room, with the woman and the diamonds; I trembled to think what might happen to me. As the steps and the voices came nearer, and the door of that outer room was opened, I made a dart for a corner of the room in which I stood—a corner across which a long curtain was hung, to form a species of wardrobe. This curtain did not reach quite to the floor, but as I slipped behind it, I saw gratefully that dresses were hung against the wall, and that one or two pairs of shoes stood on the floor; I thought it possible that my pair might pass muster with the empty ones among which they stood.

I heard the voice of the young and elegant Mr. Percy Whittaker; I heard also another voice, which I easily recognised—that of Mr. Neal Larrard. I felt that I was in a tight place indeed. Evidently, too, Mr. Whittaker was surprised to find no one in that outer room; very hurriedly, he opened the communicating door, and stepped into that inner room, in the corner of which I stood hidden.

"Funny!" I heard him say. "They told me downstairs that she had come up—the Lamb, I mean."

I was glad to know my name; even in that exciting moment I registered a mental note of it.

"A mistake, I expect," said the voice of Larrard. "By George—what a show!"

I knew that he referred to the diamonds; peeping out through a mere little moth-hole in the curtain, I saw him bending over the unconscious woman. "My boy—you've done well, indeed."

"Easy as winking," said Mr. Percy Whittaker, with a laugh. "The maid was a fool, and the night a moon-lit one; I made love to her. I flattered her (and she was rather pretty, if you come to that) and I helped her when we got ashore. Then—somehow or other—I got lost in the darkness—and the stones with me."

"Fifteen thousand—if they're worth a penny!" I heard Larrard say; and I trembled for the woman. "But why on earth is she wearing them?"

"My dear boy—that's the difficulty," said Mr. Percy Whittaker. "She was with me at Dover; we met by appointment, because I thought she might be useful. But no sooner did she clap eyes on the stones, than she must have them; she was like a mad woman, at the mere sight of them. I give you my solemn word, Larrard, she slept last night with fifteen thousand pounds about her throat—and defied me to take them from her!"

"Well—and what have you done?" asked Larrard, impatiently; and I saw his clutching fingers moving nearer to the glittering things which rose and fell with the woman's breathing.

"Given her a dose that will keep her quiet for hours. Shake

her if you like; do anything that would wake a sleeping woman; you won't wake her. The stones are ours; we will do as we like with them."

"But to get them away?" asked Larrard, looking round about him anxiously. "God, man!—have you seen the papers? Do you know how we stand?"

"I know everything," said Mr. Percy Whittaker, twisting his fair moustache. "Unless you lose your head, we can clear with the boodle within a couple of hours, and they may search London for us in vain. When Madame Jevaux wakes, she will have to explain to the hotel people; she will have but small memory of what has happened. Don't get in a funk; the Lamb is our salvation."

I was rather glad to hear that, although I wondered a little what was going to happen. Unfortunately for me their voices sank to whispers after that; and, though I strained my ears to hear what was said, I got nothing but disjointed words, which meant but little. The only thing I had to guide me was a con-stant remark by Mr. Percy Whittaker about "the roller."

Looking out through my friendly moth-hole, I saw them bend over the drugged woman, and unclasp the necklace; then I saw Mr. Larrard, with a smile of satisfaction, hold it up, and shake the wonderful things in the light. After that, they passed through into the other room, carefully closing the door behind them.

I scarcely knew what to do. To come out of that room, and confront them, was out of the question; with those jewels upon them, it would have meant a short business for me. On the other hand, I must inevitably come back from lunch, or draw suspicion upon myself by my absence. Coming out cautiously from behind the curtain, I saw another door, which was locked on the inside, and which apparently led out to the corridor of the hotel. I opened it; listened for any possible sound; and then locked it again on the outside, slipping the key into my pocket. Fortunately, I had not removed my hat or jacket; I walked up and down the corridor for a moment or two, to compose my nerves; and then opened the door of Mr. Percy Whittaker's private sitting-room, and sauntered in.

Both men looked up at me as I entered; Mr. Neal Larrard quickly and suspiciously—Mr. Percy Whittaker with his inevitable yawn. I showed some polite surprise at finding Mr. Larrard there; he smiled, and offered an explanation.

"I was not sure that you had understood my telephonic message, Miss Thorn," he said—"so I thought I would look in, to be sure that everything was right. Mr. Whittaker—everything *is* right, I believe?"

"Capital, thank you," said Mr. Percy Whittaker, genially. "Don't you worry about me." And, in a whisper, I heard him add—"Trust to the Lamb!"

As Mr. Larrard was leaving the room, he turned back, and addressed me—"Don't bother to bring the machine back to-night to the office, Miss Thorn," he said, softly; "the office will probably be closed. Take it with you to your home; and bring it in the morning—if you will be so good; cab fares, of course—and you may charge them to the office."

I wondered what had become of the diamonds; I wondered, too, which of the men would have the daring to carry that stolen fortune about with him. I was sure, in my own mind, that these were the stones for which the police were vainly hunting. Yet what could I do?

Even while I was thinking about it, I saw the sharp eyes of Mr. Percy Whittaker watching me; and I had a dreadful fear that I was colouring under his gaze. As I pulled off my jacket, I asked him quietly if he was ready to begin dictating his letters again.

"Not yet, Miss Thorn," he said slowly. "By the way, Miss Thorn—they told me in the office below that you had come up—before Mr. Larrard and I arrived. I found the door unlocked—but I didn't find you here."

I began to tremble; but my woman's wit came to the rescue. "I am very sorry to have kept you waiting, Mr. Whittaker," I said; "but, as I was rather early, and did not find you here, I slipped out again, to buy a paper. Here it is." And I held out that afternoon paper I had bought.

He looked at me steadily, and I as steadily returned his gaze. He took the paper from my hand, and glanced at it.

"You should not have left the door unfastened," he said, a little sharply.

"I am very sorry," I replied. "Did you see the account of that robbery?" I asked; and I pointed to the paper he held.

He read it through carefully, and I saw a smile flicker for a moment across his face. "That's pretty smart—isn't it?" he said. "I wonder where those stones are, Miss Thorn?"

"It would be interesting to know—wouldn't it?" I replied, calmly.

He did no more dictating that day; instead, in about an hour's time, he told me that I had better go home. "You quite understand, Miss Thorn," he said, "that you are not to go back to the office?"

"Quite," I replied. "Will you require me to-morrow?"

"No—you had better go to the office as usual," he said.

As I shifted the machine, before putting the cover on it, I heard some part of it rattle. I bent down, and looked at it; then moved the carriage backwards and forwards once or twice. Glancing up, I saw Mr. Percy Whittaker watching me.

"Well—what's the matter?" he asked.

"I'm afraid you've broken something," I said, in an injured tone. "You know you were pulling it about when I went out to lunch."

"Nothing of the kind," he replied, speaking quite roughly. "I've had nothing to do with it; I have simply played with the keys a little—that's all. Don't you worry about it, Miss Thorn; and, above all, don't be pulling it to pieces. An amateur should never meddle with a delicate thing like that. You let it alone."

I fastened up the machine—got the hotel porter to call a cab—and was driven to my home. I carried the heavy machine up to my own little room, at the top of the house, and set it down on the table. It was quite early yet, and I made up my mind to have a cup of tea at once, and make the most of my unexpected holiday by having a rest.

I was destined not to have a rest that afternoon. I had scarcely settled down before a small scrap of fire, when there came a knock at the door. Somewhat impatiently, I called out to my unwelcome visitor to enter; and the next moment my landlady appeared.

"I haven't finished my tea yet," I said, crossly.

"I wasn't meanin' to clear away, Miss," said the woman, politely. "I was on'y goin' to tell you about a curious thing that 'appened not a minute ago. A knock come at the door, and a party as looked quite the gentleman asked if Miss Smith, a typewriter, lived 'ere. I told 'im, of course, that 'e'd made a mistake, an' the on'y young lady we 'ad that was a typewriter was a Miss Thorn. 'E said 'e was very sorry to 'ave troubled me, an' went away. That was all, Miss."

For some time after the woman had gone, I sat staring at the fire, wondering what was going to happen. The thing was so obvious, on the face of it. Why should anyone come to that obscure house, and ask for a Miss Smith, a typewriter? It was obvious that the landlady would give my name; yet for what purpose was that name wanted? Was I suspected in regard to the missing diamonds?—and had I been watched, and followed? I didn't like the aspect of things at all.

Occupation is good, when one is troubled; I determined that I would not, after all, sit down idly in my room. I would at least be certain that no damage had been done to the typewriter; whatever happened I must be ready to carry on my business from day to day. I sat down at the table, and drew the machine quickly towards me.

Again that mysterious rattling. I wished, with all my heart, that Mr. Percy Whittaker were there at that moment, in order that I might tell him what I thought of him, for meddling with what he didn't understand. With a sigh of resentment, I tilted the machine back, to have a look at the levers.

Everything seemed sound; I tested them, one after the other, and found nothing wrong. Letting the machine down flat upon the table again, I heard once more that rattling.

Carefully testing every inch of it, and even removing various parts, I came at last to the conclusion that the rattling was in those little rollers or drums, round which the ribbon was wound. At a sudden remembrance which came over me of the deep interest Mr. Percy Whittaker had taken in that particular part of the machine, my face blanched, and I went hurriedly to the door, and locked it.

In five minutes I had loosened the screws, and taken out

the long steel bar which supported the drum; two more screws held the flat end of the drum in place, and these I also loosened. As the end of the little metal reel fell off, a glittering cascade of stones tumbled out on the shabby cloth which covered my table. The diamonds of the danseuse were before me.

I saw the plot in a moment. Who was to suspect a little type-writer, carrying home her machine, after the day's work, to her lodging. It was the safest and most ingenious hiding-place that could have been discovered. Yet what of that mysterious man, who had enquired at the door of the house for me, and had, in all probability, followed me. I started up, trembling with fear, as I thought of what my position would be if, at that moment, anyone could see honest little Bella Thorn, in her humble room, with all that glittering heap of diamonds before her. I took off the drum at the other end of the machine, and cascade number two tumbled out, to join the other.

In an agony of fear, I put the things back again, noticing, as I did so, how they had been torn out of the slight gold setting which had held them. Then I carefully put the drums back into their places—wound the ribbon again upon them, and restored the machine to its ordinary appearance.

I am quite sure that I did not sleep that night. A hundred times, I started up in bed in the darkness, and wondered what was going to happen to me, or what I should do, in regard to the diamonds. Do what I would, I felt that I was trapped. In the first place, the diamonds were in my possession; and I was in the possession of the gang. Who would believe me inno-cent?—I, who knew the mechanism of the machine sufficient-ly to discover the hiding place of the gems? More than that, I knew not what unknown danger I might be running into, if I attempted to betray a band of desperate men, such as Neal Larrard and his associates must be. Finally, in rather a cowardly fashion, perhaps, I determined to wait until the morning, before doing anything—perhaps in the hope that some solution of the difficulty might come.

Curiously enough, a solution awaited me at the office—although I did not know it at the time. When I arrived, accompanied by the machine, I carefully enquired of the office boy whether Mr. Larrard had arrived; he had not appeared yet. But the boy had business for me.

"A gent came just now, and left this note," he said. "Nice ole chap—very soft-spoken. Said you was to go at once, an' not lose no time."

I took the note, and opened it. It was addressed to the manager of the Secretarial Supply Syndicate, Limited, and requested that he would be good enough to send an expert typist that morning, before eleven o'clock. The address was at a huge hotel in the Strand.

I scarcely knew what to do. My brain was in a whirl; Mr. Larrard was not there; there was no one to give me orders. Afraid of myself, and afraid of everything, I determined to go to the address at once, carrying that awful machine with me.

When I arrived at the hotel, I was shewn up at once to the room; I gave no name, and asked for none. The note had simply said that a typewriter was to be sent at once. When I mentioned that in the office of the hotel, I found that I was expected, and the way was clear. In a moment or two I was in the presence of a white-haired, benevolent-looking gentleman, who, bowing profoundly, explained the situation.

"My dear lady—may I ask that you will forgive the natural

impatience of an author, to whom a sudden inspiration has come, and who would wish to set it down at once?" he asked, in a quavering, kindly voice. "I have employed a typist for some time; but my health compelled me to desist from work. Now the inspiration is upon me again, and I feel that I can resume my great story. I warn you, however," he added, with a smile, "that I may break down at any moment. Be patient with me. I am just now in the middle of a chapter; you can go on from the point at which I left off last."

He was such a restful old gentleman, and so different from anyone I had lately encountered, that it was quite a pleasure to work for him. I sat down, and laid my hands on the keys, and waited. In that quavering voice of his, he began to dictate his first passage.

"You will understand, my dear young lady, that this is the middle of a chapter," he explained, with a smile.

"Quite so," I said. And he started off:

"You put me away once; this is to pay for it. I have dogged the footsteps of the gentleman who crossed the Channel, for a day or two; I have learnt all that has happened. I start for the other side this afternoon; catch me if you can. I came out only three months ago; I have done pretty well, I think, under all the circumstances. The sparks are mine; try something neater next time. Yours—

"DANIEL MAGGS."

After that, he walked about for a little time; and then came back to me with a pathetic expression on his face.

"It's gone!" he said, in a sorrowful voice. "The inspiration has gone. I thought I really had it at last; but it's useless. Would you—would you leave me for a little while; I will try to think out how to go on. You see, this that I have just dictated to you is a letter, written by the villain of the story, in a sort of spirit of revenge. He is to send this letter to—shall we say, the hero?—and he has to think of a method to convey it to him. Leave me, I beg; come back in about half an hour."

I felt really sorry for the old gentleman; he was so simple, and so guileless, and so very different from anyone I had lately met. I told him, in all sincerity, that I was quite sure he would get over the difficulty; and he shook hands with me, and blessed me, and said I had put new heart into him. Then I went away.

When I came back, to my surprise, the people in the hotel office stared at me; they informed me that the gentleman had paid his bill, and gone. Rather bewildered, I informed them that I had left my machine in his room, and that I wanted to get it. They raised no objection whatever, and I went up.

There was the machine, standing where I had left it—even with the sheet of paper I had put in, before going, ready for the next sentence of the wonderful story. I packed up the machine, and took it away with me, back to the office. The very moment I stepped into the place, Mr. Neal Larrard, who was there, almost sprang at me.

"What on earth does this mean?" he asked, savagely. "Where have you been?"

With what dignity I could muster, I told him that I had merely answered the call of a client, in his absence. I had done my work, and then had come back again at once. Without a word, he snatched up the machine, and walked into his private office, shutting the door behind him. As I had expected, I heard him turn the key in the lock.

To my utter astonishment, in something like three minutes, the door was torn open, and he stood there, literally livid. He held a sheet of crumpled paper in his hand, and without speaking beckoned to me. I went in.

The typewriter had evidently been pulled to pieces. The ribbon hung in inky lengths over his desk; the two drums lay in pieces among his papers. But there was no glittering heap of stones.

"Where—where did you get this?" he said, in a choking voice, holding out the paper towards me. "When did you write it?"

I took the paper from his hand, and glanced over it. It was that portion of the wonderful novel which the benevolent old gentleman had dictated to me. I told Mr. Larrard so; and I trust I shall never again hear such language as that I heard then.

"Novel!—story!—are you mad?" he thundered. "Daniel Maggs—ex-convict—cleverest thief this world ever held! Can't you see that he knew everything? The stones are gone—Daniel Maggs has gone with them; and this, that you were fool enough to believe part of a novel, I find stuffed in here, in their place."

I had to play my part—difficult though it was. I looked up at him calmly, and spoke:

"Really, Mr. Larrard—I'm afraid I don't understand," I said. "And what *have* you been doing with the machine?"

He looked at me for a moment, and then laughed—a little ruefully. "Yes—I forgot," he said. "I pulled the machine to pieces, because—because I was looking for something—something important. And, by Jove!"—he held up the paper for a moment, before tearing it savagely into a dozen pieces—"I think I've found it!"

THE SPIRIT OF SARAH KEECH.

After that curious business concerning the diamonds, which had ended in so strange a fashion by the disappearance of Mr. Maggs, I confess that I waited in some trepidation (and also, perhaps, in some curiosity) to know what was to happen next. That Mr. Neal Larrard suspected me, I was sure; although I was equally sure that there were moments when he felt, on the other hand, that I was too great a fool for it to be necessary to fear me. Having always a placid exterior, I was, to all appearances, as much a machine as that at which I worked; and I think, in time, he began to cease to think that I need be considered at all.

I had had another spell of idleness, and had again got into that condition of mind when I felt I was absolutely robbing my employer, by reason of the fact that I read novels all day, and did not touch the machine at all, when I was one day surprised by the entrance of a visitor. It was such a rare event, that I closed my book hurriedly, and started to my feet in some confusion. And then faced Madame Jevaux.

She seemed to be more handsomely dressed than ever; and she gave the modest little girl sitting behind the machine a supercilious glance of contempt. Remembering how I had seen her last, and how, in a sense, I had managed to outwit her, although quite unconsciously, I felt that I cut the better figure there, handsome though she looked. Before I had time to speak, she addressed me:

"Is your—your master in?" she asked insolently.

"I'm afraid I don't understand," I said sweetly.

"Mr. Larrard," she said, with another contemptuous glance. "I want to see him."

"He is not in at present," I replied. "His movements are rather uncertain; perhaps you would like—"

"I'll wait, thank you," she said; and seated herself in the easiest chair. Having no particular reason to make a show of industry before her, I calmly resumed my book.

After a moment or two, her voice interrupted my reading. "You seem to have an easy place here?" she said.

"We're not exactly busy just now," I replied demurely.

"I wonder if you are quite what you seem," she said, after another little pause, looking at me with her handsome eyes half closed. "You seem so innocent, you know."

I scarcely knew what to say; I could only bow, in an awkward fashion, and murmur something unintelligible.

"I almost wish I had such a look as yours," she said, with a little laugh. "You see—I am labelled; all sorts of wicked things are possible, with a face like mine; yet who would suspect you? They say, however, that some of you innocent-looking ones are the most to be feared."

"There's nothing much to fear about me, I think," I said. "You see, when one has to earn one's living, it makes a difference—doesn't it? I am only a typist, at a certain salary; it is not my business to enquire about matters which do not concern me."

"Quite so," she replied, with a nod; and relapsed into silence.

Mr. Neal Larrard came in very soon after that, and was evidently somewhat disconcerted to find her there. He was not a polite man when anything put him out, or when he was dealing with those associated with him in shady transactions; and he told Madame Jevaux so strongly what he thought concerning her coming there, that I found it absolutely necessary to rattle the machine a little, in somewhat violent cleaning operations, as a reminder that he was not dealing with Madame Jevaux only.

"Don't be a fool, Neal," I heard her say in a low voice. "Do you suppose I should have come here without a good reason? Give me five minutes—and I'll convince you. There's thousands in it," she added, dropping her voice to a whisper.

"Yes—that's always the case with your schemes," he retorted, with a sneer. "However—I'll give you five minutes—not a second more."

He opened the door leading into his office, and went in first, allowing her to follow. The door was closed, and I could only hear the very faint murmur of their voices.

My small assistant, who had been furtively watching the lady as she sat in the office, had the impudence to look across at me, and wink solemnly. "Nice sort of a muvver she'd make!" he murmured. "Wouldn't trust 'er to carve the joint, I wouldn't; git into one of 'er tantrums, an' she'd about carve me, before I could run for a p'liceman. Lor'!—I do 'ope she an' the guv'nor 'as a dust-up inside!"

"You'd better get on with your work, my boy," I suggested. "You know the old motto, I suppose," I added severely.

"There's sich a lot of 'em, I get 'em mixed a bit, Miss," he replied, with a grin.

Some ten minutes later, Mr. Neal Larrard opened the door of that inner office. But a great change had come over him; and it scarcely seemed possible that the courteous gentleman, who laughingly bowed Madame Jevaux through the doorway, could be the Neal Larrard who had so contemptuously granted her a short interview a few moments ago. He was all smiles; he shook her hand warmly as she was going.

"Leave the details to me," he said, in the same low tone as that in which she had herself addressed him. "This makes up for a lot, my dear. Let me know when you think the matter is straight; and rely on me for the rest. Take care of yourself, whatever you do," he added anxiously, as he shook hands with her again.

"Trust me to do that," she replied, with a laugh.

Two days went by, and nothing was done. I began to hope that it was a scheme in which I was not to be concerned; something quite outside the actual work of the office itself. Then one afternoon, while Mr. Larrard was in the inner office, a curious blundering knock came at the door; and it was only after I had requested the knocking one to come in three separate times, that the door was opened cautiously, and the strangest couple I have ever seen entered.

It was a man and a woman; and the man came forward into the room with a little jump, having been propelled from behind by the lady. He was a little old man, with a somewhat careworn face; and with very stiff and new clothes on—clothes which might have been bought in a hurry, so badly did they fit him. He had on a very tall silk hat, with a wide brim; and this the lady dexterously snatched off his head as he entered the room, and held for him during the whole time he was there; much as though she had backed him for a sporting event of some kind, and was minding it until the contest was finished.

The lady herself was an even more extraordinary figure. She was rather bigger than the man, and more determined-looking;

when I say that she was richly dressed, that particular word requires the biggest capitals that can be given to it. She was of all the colours of the rainbow; her bonnet was absolutely indescribable; and she rustled and creaked as she walked, with the newness of every single article upon her. Feeling certain that they had made some mistake, and got to the wrong office, I rose, and asked politely who it was they wanted.

The old gentleman—being gently prodded again by the lady—discovered in one of his pockets a card; put his umbrella between his knees, while he got from another pocket his spectacle case; put the card between his teeth, while he opened the spectacle case, and got out his spectacles; returned the spectacle case to his pocket; and then began to slap himself all over, and to turn round and round, in the endeavour to find the card. The old lady taking it from between his teeth, and holding it before the spectacles, the old gentleman slowly read out the name upon it.

"Mr. Neal Larrard."

"We was asked to come an' see the gentleman," said the lady. "It's rather a private matter, Miss—very private, I might say," she added, with a glance at the little man.

"We wouldn't wish it to be known," said the man, with a glance back again.

I requested them to be seated, and went into Mr. Larrard's room. Having omitted to ask their names, I had to rely on descriptions; and I gave one of each of them, as briefly and charitably as I could. Neal Larrard began to laugh silently—shaking all over with it; then got up, and straightened his features with an effort.

"It may be necessary, Miss Thorn, that you should be present when I see these people," he said. "They are, I believe, somewhat ignorant, and it may be necessary to gain their confidence before we proceed to business."

I was about to ask what business, when I saw that hard eye of his fixed upon me; I reflected that, for the present at least, it was no affair of mine, and simply bowed.

"Send them in, please; and come in yourself when I ring," were his final instructions; and I went out, and ushered the queer-looking couple into the inner room. The last thing I saw, as I closed the door, was the old gentleman bowing jerkily, while the old lady prodded him forward, and Mr. Neal Larrard bowed gravely to them both.

I confess I was puzzled to understand what possible connection there could be between this strange-looking couple and the Secretarial Supply Syndicate; and I waited impatiently for the bell to ring. When, presently, it tinkled sharply, and I went in, I determined to preserve, if possible, that character of the "Lamb" which had been bestowed upon me; and I think to all appearances I was merely the very ordinary little typist, prepared to receive instructions, and to earn my salary as easily as possible.

The old gentleman was seated on the very edge of one chair, and the old lady, very upright and very nervous apparently, was seated on another. Behind his desk sat Mr. Neal Larrard, with a bland expression of countenance, and wearing, I thought, a very deferential air towards them. In that quick glance I had, I noticed that the old man's hands were stunted and knotted, and that the nails were worn down to the quick, as though with much labour; I thought I saw daylight on the matter.

"Miss Thorn," began Larrard, in his softest voice—"I wanted to introduce you to my friends—Mr. Jacob Pashley—Mrs.

Pashley. They have called to consult me, on the recommenda-
tion of a very old friend of mine, on a rather delicate matter;
and it occurred to me that you might like to hear what that
business is. I have no secrets from my principal secretary," he
added, turning to the old lady. "Pray be seated, Miss Thorn."

I sat down, and the old lady turned to me, and began to talk.

"You, see, my dear," she said confidentially—"me an' Jacob
'ave just come in—in the most surprisin' fashion—for a tidy bit
o' money."

"A very tidy bit, indeed," echoed the old man.

"Left to us by Jacob's great-aunt, that we 'adn't even 'eard
of, excep' by name—for years and years. More like a man than
a woman, she was—if you'll forgive me a sayin' it, Miss—as
went out somew'eres abroad, w'en old enough to know better,
an' spekilated—an' made money 'and over fist, as the sayin' is.[1]
W'en she couldn't live no longer—(bein' at that time close on
a 'underd an' one)—she died, an' left it all to Jake. An' now the
business is, we dunno' quite wot to do with it."

I could have told them, had *I* had the opportunity, that they
had better do anything with it than bring it there, or mention
it even in the presence of Mr. Neal Larrard; but I was power-
less. So I merely bowed, and murmured something about money
being a very nice thing, and glanced at Larrard. He was making
little drawings on his blotting paper with a pen, and wore an
inscrutable smile.

"It don't seem to me quite right," broke in the old man, taking

---

[1] Investment schemes designed to exploit the profit-making potential of new frontiers
    for development in the Empire or in America were not uncommon in the nineteenth
    century and figure in several novels of the period, the most detailed and scathing
    treatment of this topic being Anthony Trollope's *The Way We Live Now* (1875).

up the tale, "that me an' Jane should be simply spendin' it on ourselves—or p'raps wastin' of it fer nothin'. I'm sure I was 'appier, w'en I went out to me work every mornin', with summink in a basin fer me dinner; an' could come 'ome at night, an' smoke me pipe. We've spent all we could on clo's—an' I'm sure Jane looks a perfec' marvel, an' worth all the money; an' we're livin' at a tip-top hotel, w'ere they charges us about 'alf a crown a minute to breathe; but I feel we might be doin' more. There's such a lot of it—an' my great-aunt never left no instructions as to 'ow it was to be spent."

"You see, Miss Thorn, that is the real difficulty," broke in the quiet voice of Larrard. "Mr. and Mrs. Pashley would like to consult the dear departed."

"That is scarcely possible, I'm afraid," I said, a trifle bewildered. "She's dead, you see."

"Wot I feels, Miss," said the old lady, whom Larrard was evidently anxious should explain the matter for herself—"is that Jacob's great-aunt, 'aving bin sich a wonder in life, can't be quite as dead, in a manner o' speakin', as other people; we might be able to persuade 'er to speak to us."

"In a spirit sort o' way, Miss," added the little man. "Jane an' me 'as read a lot about spirits—an' it seems to me we might be able to git 'old of the old lady, an' ask 'er wot 'er wishes are. We've bin recommended to a lady as knows a lot about the business, an' she referred us to this gentleman, who is so good as to speak 'ighly of 'er. 'E says 'e thinks it might be managed."

"Nothing easier, I assure you," said Larrard. "I have myself studied the subject rather deeply; and I am quite convinced that it is possible to call the deceased lady—or the spirit of her—and to get from her some knowledge concerning her wishes.

Moreover, there is no harm in trying; even if we failed, you and your good wife would feel that we had done the best, and that your great-aunt would rather leave matters in your hands. You cannot do better than place yourselves in the hands of the very talented lady who sent you here; if she cannot help you, no one else can."

"I don't see why we shouldn't try," said the old lady. "You see, Miss"—she turned again to me—"me an' Jacob 'ave lived so long out of the world, in a way, that we 'aven't kept touch of all these science things,[1] excep' through the Sunday papers; an' sich a lot goes on that pore folks never 'ear of. I'm sure we're much obliged to you, sir," she added, rising—"an' we'll let you know 'ow we get on."

"Do," said Larrard, with his widest smile. "I think you'll succeed; simple faith is all that is really necessary—and you have that," he added significantly.

I saw them depart (the old lady handing Mr. Pashley his hat when they were actually outside)—and then went back to Mr. Larrard's room. He was writing at a furious rate on a sheet of note paper, and looked up frowningly as I entered.

"Well—what is it?" he asked impatiently.

"Of course, Mr. Larrard, it's nothing to do with me," I began, lamely—"but is it quite fair to tell two old people like that—?"

"Now, look here—don't interfere with what you don't understand," he said. "If you had that common sense with which I have credited you, you would know that I should scarcely

---

[1] Gallon here plays on the similarity in sound between "seance" and "science," suggesting the kind of confusion between real and bogus new knowledge among the uneducated at the turn of the twentieth century that allowed confidence tricksters such as Larrard to dupe the gullible.

have brought you in as a witness if this had been anything—well—anything not strictly right. These two old fools amuse me; why shouldn't I let them waste a little of their money on this clap-trap nonsense, if they want to do so? It'll please them, and their minds will be at rest afterwards. Now, run away, Miss Thorn—and look after your own business. Don't be so suspicious of everyone."

Feeling rather crushed, I went back to my own room. Always willing to believe, if possible, the best of everybody, I began to think that I had perhaps made much out of nothing. I began to feel, more than ever, that that was the case, when day succeeded day, and I saw nothing more of the old people, and heard nothing. At last the matter drifted out of my mind, because something more important cropped up to take its place.

Mr. Neal Larrard announced that he had taken a temporary office for a time, at which he wanted me to work. "As a matter of fact, Miss Thorn," he said, "I am thinking of having some alterations made here; more than that, there is certain work I want to do, which I cannot do if I am interrupted. I shall put in a temporary clerk here, if necessary, or perhaps merely leave the boy to answer questions. I want you to go to the new office."

"Very well, Mr. Larrard," I said. "I take the machine, of course?"

"No; that's not necessary," he said. "You will find a machine there—a very good one."

Accordingly, the next morning, on going to the office of the Syndicate, I found a note from Mr. Neal Larrard, informing me that I was to go to a certain address in Oxford Street, and was to take with me a supply of paper, and whatever else might be necessary for my work. I packed up the things, and then, on looking at the note again, saw a postscript down in one corner, which informed me that I need not go to the new office until three o'clock that afternoon. I occupied myself during the morning, and then, leaving the boy in charge, went off to the new place.

The letter had told me that the new office was on the second floor; and I climbed to that floor. The building being a tall and narrow one, wedged in between others of greater importance, there were but two doors on that floor; they were practically side by side. The first door had the words, in modest black letters on a white ground—"Madame Osborne"; obviously that could not be the new office. So I tapped at the next door, which had no name at all upon it, and a voice I recognised called to me to come in. Entering, I found Mr. Neal Larrard, smoking and looking out of a narrow window on one side of the room.

It was the queerest room imaginable. There was a thick carpet on the floor, into which one's feet seemed to sink; there was a very solid-looking typewriting table close against one wall; a couple of chairs; and that was all. The typewriting machine, which stood uncovered on the table, was of the sort to which I was accustomed. I unpinned my hat, and took it off, and prepared for work. Sitting down at the table, I did what I suppose every typist does when first sitting down; I grasped the machine at either side of the keyboard, and started to move it into a position better to suit me. To my surprise, the thing was fixed. I was bending down to peer at it, when the voice of Neal Larrard broke in rather harshly.

"Well—what's the matter with it?"

"It seems to be fixed in some way, Mr. Larrard," I said.

"Well—what if it is?" he exclaimed impatiently. "Can't you work as well at it; what do you want to pull it about for?"

"There is no necessity to move it, of course," I said, rather stiffly; and seated myself in readiness for whatever he might dictate.

"You're rather good, Miss Thorn, at keeping your own counsel," said Larrard, in a low voice. "I want you clearly to understand, this afternoon, that I am embarking on a business which it is not necessary to explain. If my sentences are disjointed—it need not trouble you."

At that moment a bell tinkled quickly in the room. I jumped, and looked round in surprise; I could not see a bell anywhere. I was just about to speak, when I felt the heavy hand of Neal Larrard on my shoulder.

"Write," he whispered—"quickly!"

My hands were on the keys; quite mechanically they followed the words he spoke—

"Yes—I am the spirit of Sarah Keech."

I wondered if Mr. Neal Larrard happened to be going in for literature; but, of course, I said nothing. After a moment or two, the bell rang again; and once more Neal Larrard spoke, and the keys moved sharply under my touch.

"You have nothing to fear," I wrote as he dictated—*"you are in the hands of good friends. Do all they suggest; they will advise you for the best."*

"This machine works very stiffly, Mr. Larrard," I said, looking up at him.

"So that it works at all, there's nothing for you to trouble about, Miss Thorn," he said sharply. "Please attend to what I am saying."

Another pause—and then I heard the tinkle of the bell again. Instantly Mr. Larrard spoke.

"There is a big dark man, whom you have consulted; trust him to any extent; if he advises you what to do with the money—do it, without question."

Of course I could not make head nor tail of what I was writing; I was simply doing what I was told. And hard work it was for my fingers, for the keys wanted much thumping before they would go down fully. There was another, and a shorter pause; then the tinkle of the bell; and another sentence.

"Yes—I am quite happy; much happier than I expected to be. Don't worry about me. The same medium can call me at any time. Good-bye!"

The bell rang no more. I sat before the machine for a moment or two, expecting further work. Presently Neal Larrard came across to where I sat, and told me to take the paper out of the machine; I did so, and he read it carefully through. Then he folded it up, and put it in his pocket.

"A very successful piece of work, Miss Thorn," he said quietly. "Wait a few moments; and then you can go."

"Is that all you want, Mr. Larrard?" I asked.

"That is all, Miss Thorn—thank you," he replied, with a smile. "I'll give you a holiday to-morrow morning; you need not go to the office; come here at three o'clock instead, and you will find me. Put on your hat; that is all for to-day."

Now, I am a very methodical sort of person, and I like always to be prepared for my work; I find that nothing irritates a man so much as having to wait, while a nervous typist oils the machine, and generally rubs it up, and then inserts the first sheet of paper. Therefore, while Mr. Larrard stood, watching, I carefully went over the typewriter, and then slipped in a sheet of paper, ready for the morrow. That done, I resumed my hat and jacket; and he let me out on to the staircase. It being then past my usual hour for leaving the office, I went straight off home, wondering if any other girl in London had so little to do for so much money.

I had a late breakfast the next morning, and found myself still pondering over that business of the previous afternoon. There was nothing with which I could connect it; yet it occurred to me that it was absurd that a man should be paying three pounds a week to a typist to write three or four sentences in an afternoon. I tried to dismiss the matter from my mind, but failed to do so.

I got to the new office rather early that afternoon; principally, I think, because I had a conscientious feeling that I ought not to be idle under all the circumstances. Going up to the second floor of that house in Oxford Street, I found the door locked; I was turning away, when a woman with a bunch of keys jangling in her hand approached me. I imagined her to be the housekeeper of the premises, and she looked at me narrowly for a moment.

"Was you wantin' to go in, Miss?" she asked, selecting one particular key from the bunch.

I explained briefly that I had been at work in the office on the previous day, and that I was afraid I was a little early. Evidently the woman was reassured, for she unlocked the door, and let me in.

It wanted still some quarter of an hour of the time appointed by Mr. Neal Larrard. Inwardly congratulating myself upon the fact that he would find I was only too ready to be punctual, I removed my hat, and sat down in my usual place at the table. And then a weird and startling thing happened.

The typewriter began to work! I saw first one key go down, and then another; then I hurriedly pushed back my chair, and got as far away from the unholy thing as I could. I confess I was horribly frightened; key after key went down, with a quick snap, and the carriage of the machine moved slowly and jerkily along. Then all at once it stopped, and I crept slowly back to it.

I looked at the desk closely—even went down on my knees on the floor, to see if I could peer underneath; it was all solid and immovable. Then, with a sort of dreadful feeling upon me that I was probing secrets I did not understand, I pulled out the sheet of paper I had put in on the previous day. And here is the strange thing I read:

"jJaNe paSHlYe pARagoNhOTeL wesT mInsteR."

It took me a moment or two to spell the thing out; when I had got it fully, I confess I was startled again. Put out in proper form, it of course read as follows:

"Jane Pashley, Paragon Hotel, Westminster."

My mind jumped in a moment to that extraordinary figure of the old lady, who had called upon Mr. Neal Larrard in his office, and had expressed a desire to communicate with the great-aunt of the curious old gentleman who accompanied her. At the same time, I was more puzzled than ever to understand what it meant. Was it possible that Neal Larrard possessed powers of which I knew nothing; was it possible that within the past five minutes the extraordinary dead woman—great-aunt to Mr. Jacob Pashley—had been playing tricks with the machine, and absolutely writing on it with spirit fingers? I shuddered a little, as I looked at the square metal thing with its gleaming white keys. Hearing a sound outside in the corridor, however, I hurriedly crumpled up the paper, and thrust it into my pocket; when, a moment later, Mr. Neal Larrard entered, I was hanging up my coat, in the most innocent fashion, and preparing for work.

"How did you get in here?" he asked, looking at me suspiciously.

"I met a woman—the housekeeper, I suppose—outside; and she let me in—not a moment ago," I said innocently. "I thought you would like me to be ready, Mr. Larrard."

"Oh—certainly—certainly," he replied lamely. "Quite right, Miss Thorn."

I said nothing to him about that extraordinary writing which the machine had done without apparent assistance; although I could not explain it to myself, I determined to watch, and endeavour to discover something, before speaking of the matter at all. After a moment or two, during which I had slipped in another sheet of paper, I heard the bell tinkle, and sat ready, with my hands touching the keys.

It would take too long to detail all the messages I wrote that afternoon; the spirit of Sarah Keech (whoever she might be) was referred to again and again; and she appeared to give instructions concerning the disposal of property, and of very considerable sums of money. When what appeared to me to be a very useless afternoon's work had been completed, Mr. Neal Larrard, apparently very well satisfied, once again dismissed me.

As I came out of the place, I saw a tall woman standing in the doorway leading to the street, buttoning her glove. She glanced round, to look at something passing in the street, and I saw in a moment that it was Madame Jevaux. She did not see me; before I went out she had gathered up her skirts in one well-gloved hand, and stepped into the street.

I began to put things together, although I was still far from the truth. I began to wonder what Madame Jevaux was doing at that place; Madame Jevaux, who had been concerned already in two extremely shady matters to my own knowledge. Again, the name of Pashley brought back to my remembrance that curious interview in the office of Mr. Neal Larrard.

The rest of the day was mine; scarcely knowing why I did so, I started off in the direction of Westminster; and presently, in a quiet little street there, I found the Paragon Hotel. With my mind fully made up, I walked in, and enquired for Mrs. Pashley.

The old lady came out within a minute, and greeted me effusively. She kissed me heartily in the hall of the hotel—addressed me, in her simple homely fashion, as "My dear"; and insisted that I should come up to their private sitting room, and see "Jacob." So I went up, and had tea with them.

Gradually I drew them on to tell me what they had been doing during the past few days. As I asked my judicious questions, I saw them glance from one to the other; and then the old lady burst out in a sort of rapturous whisper.

"My dear—me an' Jacob feels that we ought to tell yer," she began. "Which I may say at once that 'is great-aunt as bin fetched up, as I might say."

"Fetched up?" I asked, in some perplexity.

"Yes, Miss," said the little man, continuing the story. "We found a very nice lady, as knew the business backwards. Got all the latest ideas too. Used one of them things like I saw at your place, w'en me an' Jane came up to see Mr. Larrard; like a small pianner—on'y with round keys."

"You mean a typewriter," I said.

"That's it, Miss," broke in the old lady. "One o' them things that keeps on tip-tapping, an' gits it off on a bit o' paper as clear as print. Although 'ow Sarah Keech ever learnt it in them parts beats me!"

Sarah Keech was the name I had typed at the dictation of Mr. Neal Larrard on the previous day; I listened eagerly for what was to follow.

"You must know, Miss," went on the old lady—"that me an' Jacob, wishin' to ask Sarah Keech (as died in 'er flower, so to speak, at a 'undred an' one) wot was 'er wishes concernin' the property, went to a Madame Osborne, at a 'ouse in Oxford Street. Fixed up in the lady's room was one of those things you calls a typewriter. Well, Madame Osborne (tall an' dark, an' very 'andsome she was, I'm sure; as Jacob 'ere couldn't keep, 'is eyes orf 'er!) calls out sudden fer Sarah Keech. Then that there blessed thing with the white keys begins to tap; movin' of itself, in a way that made me flesh creep. All sorts o' questions Madame asked; an' each one was answered, afore you could wink, on the machine. Then w'en it was all over, Madame Osborne lifts out the paper, and passes it to me. 'I don't want you to think,' she says, 'that there's any deception; read it for yourselves.' An' there it was, my dear, jist as Sarah Keech 'ad said it, an' spelt lovely; w'ich I never knew 'er to be no scholar, particularly in life, but doubtless improved in the last month or two."

"Have you the paper that was taken from the machine?" I asked.

"Certainly, my dear; here it is," said the old lady, fumbling in her pocket; and to my utter astonishment she brought out the exact replica of what I had written on the typewriter, at Mr. Neal Larrard's dictation, the previous afternoon. While I puzzled over it, the old gentleman suddenly flung a ray of light on to the business.

"We was there too early this arternoon, Miss," he said, with a chuckle—"an' bless you, Jane 'ere, 'oo 'asn't got no more reverence for the departed than a p'liceman, must go a writin' 'er name an' address on the machine. Sits down, she does, an' spells it out lovely—'Jane Pashley, Paragon Hotel, Westminster.' The letters was a bit up an' down, an' all sorts o' sizes, but plain to be read," he added, with pride.

"In which room did you write that?" I asked.

"Which room, Miss? W'y—in Madame Osborne's, of course!" exclaimed the old lady. "That's w'ere the typewriter is."

Two facts became apparent to me; the first, that the Pashleys had received on their typewriter the messages I had written on mine; the second, that I had received the ill-written name and address on my typewriter which they had written on theirs. A sudden thought occurring to me, I turned to the old lady quickly.

"I'm so glad to know that you have heard from Mr. Pashley's great-aunt," I said—"because it puts everything so much more clearly before you—doesn't it? I want to tell you, by the way, that Mr. Larrard has heard from Madame Osborne; and she would like you to be at her room to-morrow half an hour earlier. Can you manage that?"

"Certainly, Miss," responded the old lady. "Our time's all our own, you know."

"And please don't say anything about having seen me," I suggested. "You see, Mrs. Pashley, I'm only a typist; and it might be thought that I was taking a liberty in coming to see people like you. So please don't say anything to anyone."

The old lady assured me that she perfectly understood, and the old gentleman, by way of expressing how completely he had grasped the situation, shook my hand many times, and winked solemnly. Then I went out of the Paragon Hotel, in a very thoughtful frame of mind.

I reached the building in Oxford Street before two o'clock the next afternoon; I knew that the Pashleys could not be expected to arrive before half-past two. I found my friend the housekeeper, and greeted her smilingly; she let me into Mr. Larrard's office at once, and stood for a moment to chat; I distinctly gave her encouragement.

"Funny work, yours, Miss," she suggested. "Seem to be used everywheres nowadays; they've got one of them typewriters next door." She jerked her thumb in the direction of Madame Osborne's room as she spoke.

"Indeed," I said. "What does she want it for?"

"Oh—some 'anky-panky, I'll be bound. Reads 'ands—an' all that kind o' bunkum, Miss," said the woman. "Like to 'ave a look?" she asked, as a sort of invitation.

"Very much indeed," I said; and we went together into Madame Osborne's room.

It was a much larger room than the other, and the one window was darkened, while the walls were hung with heavy curtains. The only light at all came from a small electric lamp, half hidden, which shed a light straight down on to the keys of a typewriter standing on a table flat against the partition wall. There were three or four chairs, and a small table, in the room in addition. I was moving across towards the typewriter, when, just at the edge of the table, my foot struck against a slight projection under the carpet. Pressing on it with one foot, I heard a bell ring sharply in the next room, the door of which had been left open. It gave the same quick tinkling sound that I had heard before, while seated at the typewriter, waiting for Mr. Larrard to dictate to me.

"Some people I know are coming up this afternoon to see Madame Osborne," I said, as we turned to go—"and they won't want to wait outside, if she should happen to be late. Will you let them in; they won't do any damage, if they stop here for five minutes."

"Certainly, Miss," said the housekeeper, her large hand closing promptly over the two half crowns I slipped into her palm. "And if you'd like to 'ave a look at the machine for a minute, Miss—"

I went across to the machine, and essayed to lift it; it was fixed, like the one in the other room. A rapid calculation of distances showed me, moreover, that this particular machine was placed against the dividing wall between the two rooms, in such a position that it was absolutely with its back to the machine on the other side of that wall; the light was fully on, above the keys, and, slipping my hand round behind it, I came upon a set of long slim steel levers, running right up against the wall. More than that, they appeared to go through the wall itself, or rather through the curtain which shrouded it.

I began to understand very clearly indeed. I turned to the waiting housekeeper, and thanked her. "You will look after my friends when they come to see Madame Osborne," I said. "And please say nothing about me."

I went back to the other room, and examined the machine at which I had been working. I had noticed, before leaving Madame Osborne's room, that there was a sheet of paper ready fixed in the machine; I slipped one into my own. Then I began carefully to examine the typewriter in every part.

It was firmly screwed to the table; but, by bending down, and peering underneath, I saw that a most ingenious arrangement of thin steel levers had been fixed, as in the machine in the other room, to the bars which supported the keys, and by means of which the type was set in motion. Having no knowledge of mechanics, it is impossible for me to describe all the mechanism; but in a little place in the wall, which was shrouded, as in the other room, by a curtain, was a curious arrangement of cranks, so fixed that when I pressed down a key in the machine in Neal Larrard's room, the lever which went through the wall operated on the identical key in the other machine. I began to understand how it was that the spirit of Sarah Keech had managed to work the typewriter so successfully. I listened at the door, with my mind firmly made up, until I heard the garrulous tones of the housekeeper outside, and the closing of Madame Osborne's door. Then I flew to the typewriter, and began.

"Is that my dear Jacob Pashley?" I wrote (and I hope the old gentleman has forgiven me the liberty long since). *"I am his great-aunt—Sarah Keech. He is being swindled; all the money I saved so carefully for him will be stolen, unless he is careful. I have not really spoken to you before this; I am speaking now. By my hundred-and-one years, I charge you to keep the money I gave you in your own hands: to spend it as you like; to do some good with it. Put this paper in your pocket, Jacob Pashley, and run away from this house with your wife as quickly as you can; if I hear of any more of this nonsense, I'll come back, and haunt you. Go away!"*

I put my ear to the wall, close against the back of the machine; through the curtains, closely as they were packed, I heard the roller of the other machine move, as the paper was pulled out. A few minutes afterwards, that other door was stealthily opened; and, peering through the door of the room in which I was, I saw the old couple go on tip-toe down the stairs, without ever once glancing back. And that was the last I ever saw of them.

Mr. Neal Larrard waited impatiently for half an hour that afternoon, whilst I sat demurely at the keys; then he went out, and had a conference with Madame Osborne in whispers on the staircase. Of course, it was not for me to say anything, and the paper on which I had written in my machine was safely tucked away in my pocket. When Mr. Neal Larrard finally dismissed me, evidently feeling that the game was hopeless, I asked quietly if he would want me to come to that office again.

"I don't think so," he said. "There's been a little—a little leakage somewhere," he muttered, half to himself. "I wish I could find out where it was."

But he never did find out, and I have a fancy that I successfully laid the ghost of Sarah Keech that afternoon.

THE SAVING OF CURLY-HEAD.

It may readily be supposed, and has, in fact, already been hint-ed, that at the office of the Secretarial Supply Syndicate, we had, from time to time, some queer visitors. Now and then, of course, a legitimate visitor, who really meant innocent busi-ness only, would make his appearance, and would be smilingly received by Mr. Neal Larrard (probably in the hope that other sort of business would be forthcoming).

In most cases, however, these visitors were informed, with many regrets, that we were so extremely busy that we hadn't a secretary to spare. In other cases the visitor—probably recom-mended from one of those outside sources of which only Mr. Neal Larrard knew—was detained, and a little real business done. As a matter of fact, however, I had found myself growing into such a suspicious state, that I should have looked upon the mild-est man or woman that ever breathed as a person with a criminal intent; so that I at last gave up trying to diagnose between the sheep and the goats at all, and took things as they came.

My first introduction to Mr. Augustus Kealing was one I shall not easily forget. Having nothing to do in the office, as usual, I was deeply immersed in the pages of—never mind what book; I have no wish to give a gratuitous advertisement to anyone—and I dropped the book in a hurry, at the sound of a cough right beside me. Twisting round, with something of a cry, I saw a very thin young man, with very light hair parted in the middle—eyes much too near together to be satisfactory—and a mouth which was one continual grin. How in the world he had got into the place, without my hearing him, I could not then understand; later on, when I came to know how silently he could move, I understood better. For in some way he had opened the door of the office, and closed it again; and had glided into a seat beside me, before I knew that he was there at all.

I was too astonished to speak; he saved me the trouble. Running one long thin hand gently round and round his silk hat, and fixing me with his narrow little eyes, he spoke.

"Oh, I beg your pardon, I'm sure," he said; and his voice was little more than a whisper. "I knocked, you know" (which I did not believe for a moment) "and I could make no one hear. I do hope that I am not interrupting your work."

"Not in the least, thank you," I said. "What is your business?" I spoke sharply, because I did not like the look of the man.

"I have been recommended to—to the Syndicate," he said, in that same ghastly whisper. "A Mr.—Mr. Larrard, I believe—"

"That is the manager, certainly," I replied. "Do you wish to see him?"

"If it is not disturbing anyone the least little bit," he said. "Of course, I would not wish for a moment—"

"If you come here on business," I said, more sharply than ever—"you have a right to take up our time, I suppose. What name shall I say?"

He dived one thin hand into his waistcoat pocket, and wriggled a card out of it, much as though he were performing a species of conjuring trick. In long, attenuated letters, as thin as himself, I read his name—"Mr. Augustus Kealing."

Mr. Larrard, after attentively regarding the card for a few moments, in an evident endeavour to call something to mind, asked me to send the gentleman in. I did so, and felt very relieved at getting rid of him.

Quite half an hour elapsed, before I heard or saw anything more of the visitor; then Mr. Neal Larrard's bell rang sharply, and I went in. As I opened the door, I saw that both the visitor and the manager were finishing a laugh at some joke they had had together; it had been so good a joke that they had not had time to compose their features before my entry; in fact, they did not trouble very much to do so after I was in the room.

"Providence does arrange these things sometimes—doesn't it?" asked Larrard, addressing the visitor.

"It certainly seems like it," said Mr. Kealing, with another grin.

"Did you ring, Mr. Larrard?" I asked demurely.

"Yes, Miss Thorn. Sit down, please," said Larrard. He seemed to be in a remarkably good humour, and I felt that there was mischief brewing, on that account. "This is Mr. Kealing, who has been recommended to us. He is anxious to engage—on behalf of an elderly lady—his aunt—a secretary and amanuensis.[1] The duties, he tells me, are very light—"

"Oh—extremely light," broke in Mr. Kealing. "Merely a fad, if I may venture to say so, on the part of my esteemed aunt. She—she's a poetess, you know—writes verses."

"Indeed?" I said.

"There are also other light duties to be performed, Miss Thorn," said Larrard, busy with a pen on the blotting paper before him—"pleasant duties. There is a small boy—as a

---

[1]   A person who writes from dictation or copies manuscripts; a literary assistant.

matter of fact, the half-brother of Mr. Kealing here—in whom he is very deeply interested."

I was glad to think, at that moment, as I glanced at the visitor, that he did not pay me the compliment of being interested in me in quite the same fashion; for that smile of his was deadly, and made me shudder to see it.

"Yes—I am most anxious about the dear child," said Augustus Kealing, in his soft whisper.

"He is only a very little fellow, Miss Thorn, and will require a few simple lessons at your hands; you won't mind combining your secretarial duties with that, I am sure?"

"Not at all," I said. "If the other duties are so light, it will help to fill out the time."

"You know, Miss Thorn,—we live a long way away," said Mr. Kealing, turning his expansive grin full upon me. "A dreary sort of place, I'm afraid, for a young lady; on the coast—Cornwall, you know."

"I am very fond of the sea," I said.

"That's fortunate," he responded. "I don't think we need detain you any longer, Miss Thorn," he added— "there are one or two details I have to settle with Mr. Larrard. And I'm delighted to know that the sweet little boy will be in such good hands."

Mr. Augustus Kealing worked his way out through the office a little later—bowing to me as he passed my desk; at the door, however, he came back for a moment, to speak in a confidential tone.

"I shall not, I fear, see you down in Cornwall, Miss Thorn," he said—"I am going abroad almost immediately. But I would like to say again how glad I am that you are going down there. You will like the child—and I am most anxious for his welfare—most anxious."

Then he was gone, and I heard Larrard's bell ring for me. I went in, and found him pacing about the room, with the smile gone from his face, and in its place a very determined expression. I closed the door, and he began to give me my instructions.

"It rather looks, Miss Thorn," he said, in a low voice, "as though this might be a long business. Speaking confidentially, it is evident that this aunt—a Miss Dobbs—fancies herself to be a literary character; all she will want to do is to spout bad verse to you, I imagine, in inspired moments, and leave you pretty much to yourself when she is not inspired. The child need not trouble you very much; he is only a little fellow, and will not, I suppose, be learning much more than the alphabet and a few things of that sort. It's a big house—plenty of servants—and a reliable nurse to look after the child. And it will give you a holiday."

"You are very good, Mr. Larrard," I said.

"I have put the address down here; and you mustn't be startled at the name of the house. They get all sorts of queer names in remote districts. It's called 'Smuggler's End,' and stands actually on the coast. You had better start to-morrow morning; and I will, of course, provide you with sufficient funds for the journey."

But for the fact of that dreadful face of Mr. Augustus Kealing, and but for my very natural suspicions regarding the Secretarial Supply Syndicate, I should have looked upon the matter as innocent enough. An old woman, who wanted to dictate her poetical effusions—a young child, to be taught for perhaps an hour a day; what could possibly be wrong with that? At the same time, I fully made up my mind to be watchful, and to suspect everyone until I discovered that they were innocent.

I started the next morning on my journey. For obvious reasons, I must not write down here the name of the town to which I went; suffice it that I found a carriage waiting for me, and was driven some five or six miles, until I heard the sound of the sea booming in my ears. And there before me was the most gaunt-looking and weird old house I ever remember to have seen.

It was perched on the very top of the cliff, and almost overhung the sea. A high stone wall enclosed the grounds by which it was surrounded on three sides; on the fourth side—that which overlooked the sea—the walls actually met the house; I discovered afterwards that a narrow road ran along the top of the cliff, and was bounded on the one side by the actual wall of the house; it was a private road, and apparently very seldom used. Thus it will be seen that, save for that road, the wall of the house and the wall of the cliffs formed one straight precipice.

I only discovered that afterwards; I was too much interested in the people within the walls to think about anything else. I was very kindly received by Miss Dobbs, to whom I was to act as secretary. She was a large lady, with what might have been termed by her friends a dreamy aspect; I should have called it sleepy. She evidently wore very soft shoes; and she went about the house with a sort of bumping motion, that shook her fat cheeks considerably as she moved. I sat down that night to dinner with her alone, save for the presence of a couple of servants.

The furniture of the house had at one time been very good; when I saw it, it was old, and had been badly used. The great rooms had a forlorn and dreary appearance, as though no one ever lived in them.

Miss Dobbs talked poetry steadily throughout dinner, and gave me to understand that she was at that time engaged on a tremendous work, which would make for her undying fame; she had felt, however, that the labour of writing was too much for her, and that her thoughts would flow more freely if she simply sat still, and poured those thoughts out, whilst I wrote them down. (Perhaps I may mention that, on the one or two occasions when she adopted this method—generally after a very hearty meal—she was asleep in less than five minutes; so that my labours were considerably lightened.)

I was shewn to my room that night—and I honestly think that it was the dreariest room in all that dreary house. It had, as its chief article of furniture, a huge old four-post bedstead; the whole thing was black, and the curtains were dingy with age. When I found courage to undress, I discovered that my small person occupied about a tenth part of it; and that I lay, as it were, in a very ocean of bed clothes. But the sound of the sea lulled me to sleep, and I slept heavily.

I awoke while it was very early; and after the first moment of surprise at finding myself in a strange room, I recollected the events that had brought me there, and got up. There was not a sound in the house, but the sun was shining brightly in at the window, and it tempted me out. I dressed, and started on a tour of exploration, determining to move quietly, so that I might not disturb anyone.

I had come up many stairs on the previous night, and my room was at the end of a long corridor, out of which other doors opened. At the end of that corridor was a huge window, opening, in lattice fashion, in the middle, and inwards. The bottom of these glass doors—for such they were—was actually within some eighteen inches of the ground;[1] I concluded, as I got nearer to them, that they were never opened. I looked out, when I reached them, and saw below me the splendid stretch of sea, far out to the horizon, with the sun sparkling upon it. It looked so good, and seemed so near, that I began to fumble with the catch of the window, to open it.

The catch was rusty, and there was, in addition, a bar across it; however, I managed to unfasten it, and drew the two doors inwards. Holding to them, and feeling the clear morning air on my face, and scenting the delicious smell of the sea, I leaned out a little, and looked down.

I own I turned giddy. The window was a considerable height from the ground, and only that strip of road broke the sheer precipice, which went right down to the water; but for that, there was nothing to break a fall; and that mere eighteen inches of woodwork, against which my knees were pressed, was nothing at all. I drew back hurriedly, and closed the window, and fastened it securely.

The muse was coy that morning, and Miss Dobbs decided that she would not work. In order, as I more than suspected, to get rid of me, she rang the bell, and asked that Master Charles might be sent in.

There came in, a moment or two later, the most beautiful little boy I have ever seen. He must have been between four and five years of age; he had wide-open clear blue eyes, and naturally curling soft fair hair rumpled all over his head; he was exactly like a picture I remember to have seen in an old

---

[1] By "ground," Gallon apparently refers here to the floor inside the house. Two paragraphs below there is another reference to the window being "a considerable height from the ground" (rather than eighteen inches), this second use of ground referring to the road outside the window.

house to which I once went. He was evidently a very shy and nervous sort of boy; he came up to me frankly enough, after a little hesitation; yet he spoke in the subdued tones that seemed natural in that house, but unnatural to a child. Miss Dobbs suggested that I should take him away, and make friends with him. So I took him by the hand, and we walked out of the room together.

In the corridor outside I almost fell over a woman, who was standing very erect outside the door. She gave me a stern glance, that seemed to take in my whole figure, and character, and everything else, in one sweeping look; and then, seizing the boy's other hand, dragged him roughly away from me. She was marching down the corridor, with the boy in tow, when I felt that it was time to assert myself, and went rapidly after her. She turned as she heard my pursuing footsteps, and faced me defiantly.

"What do you want?" she asked, in a hard voice.

"I want that child," I replied. "I don't know who you are— but I may tell you that I am here to look after him, and to act as his governess. Under any circumstances, you've no right to behave in that fashion," I added.

She was an elderly woman, of a hard and forbidding aspect; yet at that moment I saw in her face something that made me respect her—some touch of that fierce love that makes the tigress fight for her young.

"Who sent you to this house?" she asked.

"Mr. Augustus Kealing originally arranged that I—"

She gave a sort of sob, and seemed, in one wild moment, to beat me off with her hands. Remembering my suspicion of that Mr. Kealing, I approached her gently, as she turned away from me, and spoke quietly.

"Come—I don't know your name—but won't you look at me? Do you think I am likely to do the child any harm? Look at me!"

She turned me round, so that the light from a window fell upon my face. The child was looking at us wonderingly. As the woman gazed at me, I saw her features slowly relax; then she bent her head.

"I—I ask your pardon, Miss; but I'm suspicious of everyone," she said, in a whisper. "If you should be going with Master Charlie into the grounds, maybe I could come with you, and—and tell you."

Wondering a little, I agreed to the plan; and we went down into the great neglected garden which spread round the house. I seated myself on a bench there; and the woman stood, in a stern, uncompromising fashion, before me, with her arms folded. The child was playing about on the grass near at hand.

"My name is Blades," she began. "I've been with the boy since his birth; I was with his mother years before that. She was the young wife of an old man; they are both dead. That child—caring for nothing but the sunshine and the butterflies at this moment—is heir to one of the greatest properties in England. The old man—his father—loved his child-wife, and left everything to this baby; the other son—a mean and shiftless creature, would kneel before you one day, and stab you in the back the next—is left with a few hundreds a year."

"You mean Mr. Augustus Kealing?" I asked.

She nodded grimly. "That tender little life is at the mercy of that half-brother, and of any others who might benefit, if the life was crushed out," she went on. "Miss Dobbs"—she gave a contemptuous snap to her fingers—"doesn't care that;

I am the only one to stand between the child and any danger that threatens. So you'll understand, Miss, why I was suspicious—won't you?"

I assured her that I understood, and that I was glad to think that anyone so loyal was there, to guard the child. Thinking over the matter deeply, while she stood silent, I began to have a hair-raising feeling that my responsibility in this matter was greater than any I had had yet. Mr. Neal Larrard did not concern himself in anything of this sort without cause; I thought of the great fortune that belonged to this child; I recognised how small a life it was, and what a strange and lonely place we were in. I think a sort of desperate prayer went up in my heart that we might beat Mr. Augustus Kealing at his own game—although I did not quite see how it was to be done.

The bench on which I sat faced towards the sea; that is to say, the high wall, which at that point joined the house, bounded the road that wound along the top of the cliffs. And over the top of that wall, at the very moment that the woman Blades had ceased speaking, I saw appear the head of Augustus Kealing. On the face was the same evil grin; but the head disappeared so suddenly, as the eyes looked for a moment into mine, that I had a feeling I must be mistaken. Blades had her back to the wall, and so saw nothing.

Day succeeded day, until three or four had gone past; and nothing happened. I don't suppose that twenty lines of the immortal poem were written; more than once I amused myself by sticking in a line or two on my own account, after Miss Dobbs had fallen asleep. Then, on about the fourth day, something very curious occurred.

At one end of the garden was an old disused well, with a

flat square stone covering the top of it. My attention was first drawn to it by the child, who was jumping about, and stamping his feet on the stone, to wake the echoes far below him. We sat down there for a long time, and then went back to the house; and I thought no more about the matter. The boy occasionally wandered out into the grounds; even Blades felt that he was perfectly safe there, because they were enclosed, and there was no way out of them.

On the next morning I went out very early—before breakfast, in fact—and wandered up and down in the garden, thinking and wondering when the first attack was to be made. I had heard nothing from Mr. Neal Larrard, and the silence was more suspicious, to my mind, than anything else. Turning mechanically in my walk, I strolled in the direction of the old well—not with any thought of it in my mind, but because it came quite naturally in my walk round the place. I had reached the very edge of it, before I started back, with a little cry. The stone had been flung back on to the turf, and the round dark wicked mouth of the thing was exposed!

I knelt down beside it, and dropped a stone in. I heard the boom, far down below, when the stone at last struck water; I shuddered, and drew away. Then, regaining my courage a little, I dragged the stone back into its place, and set it firmly over the mouth of the well. And I said nothing to Blades or anyone else.

The next strange thing happened that very morning. I had gone out with the child alone into the grounds, carrying a book in my hand; the boy was trotting up and down in the drive which led up to the house, while I sat engaged with my book. Suddenly I heard the great bell at the gates clang, and a moment or two later a servant came hurrying down from the house, and pulled them open. A dog-cart[1] swept in through the gates, and in that dog-cart sat Mr. Neal Larrard. I was so surprised at seeing him, that for a moment I was struck motionless; and in that moment everything happened.

Now, I am perfectly prepared to swear—on oath, if necessary—that the horse driven by Larrard came in quite quietly through the gates; I am also perfectly prepared to swear that the moment it had passed those gates it began to plunge horribly. The whip that Larrard held came down heavily across the creature's head; the animal reared, swerved, and bore straight down on the child.

In less time than it takes to write, something had darted out from the trees behind me; had got to the boy; and was holding him in an embrace which put her own body between him and the horse. It was Blades—and she was down in a moment—under the animal, as it seemed—and then up again, staggering, with the child in her arms. And the picture I saw was Larrard, white as death, and hatless, holding the horse; Blades—whiter still—holding the child, and facing him. Then I knew that the real struggle had begun.

Mr. Neal Larrard was horribly distressed at what might have been a very serious accident; he patted and caressed the small boy (who would have none of him), and complimented Blades upon her extreme bravery. He had been down in that part of the country on business; and it had suddenly occurred to him that it might be well if he called at Smuggler's End, to see how Miss Thorn was getting on. He would only remain an hour or so, and pay his respects to Miss Dobbs—and then would return.

---

[1] A small two-wheeled horse-drawn open carriage, originally with a compartment under the seat for dogs.

Then it was that Miss Dobbs presented a difficulty. Mr. Neal Larrard was enchanted with the house—enchanted with everything, in fact; more than all else, he admired Miss Dobbs' poetry. She asked him to lunch; and after lunch changed her usual habits so much, as to remain awake, and read him the whole of the first book. In a most surprising manner (I couldn't have done it), he kept awake also, and kept on pleading for more. Thus it happened that, in the most natural fashion in the world, he stayed for an early dinner; and then found (having sent the horse and trap back to the town) that there was no way of getting back that night; even if he availed himself of the carriage, he would arrive only to find that the last train had gone hours before.

What was to be done? Mr. Neal Larrard buttoned his coat, and smilingly expressed his intention to walk down to the town, and put up at the inn. Miss Dobbs, with more reading of poetry in her mind, declared that such a thing was out of the question, and that Mr. Larrard must occupy a room in that great house. He protested—but in vain; a room was prepared for him; and I, setting my teeth, prepared also for a sleepless night.

Without alarming her more than could be avoided, I approached Blades. I discovered where she slept; I knew already where the boy slept. To my horror, I found that she had been turned out of her room, next to the boy's, to make way for Mr. Larrard; it was a comfortable room, and Mr. Larrard, having seen it, had expressed admiration for it. That was sufficient; Miss Dobbs decided that he should have it.

As ill-luck would have it, the only other room ready was on the floor above; and to this, despite the pleadings of Blades, Miss Dobbs despatched her. Blades gave me a meaning glance, full of entreaty, and I determined to watch carefully. The boy was put to bed in the usual course, and I saw no more of Blades that night. Miss Dobbs, Neal Larrard, and I sat talking, in a desultory fashion, for an hour or two longer.

I suppose I am not so cunning as I should be; at all events, I was outwitted that night. Miss Dobbs was so pleased at the effect her poetry had had, that she became quite genial and convivial; and insisted, at the last moment, that wine and biscuits should be brought before we retired. The wine came up, and three glasses were filled. I put my lips to mine, and then—not wishing to drink any more—turned away, and picked up a book. Miss Dobbs was falling asleep, and Larrard was sipping his wine, and looking thoughtfully at it, while he still prosed on about poetry generally, and Miss Dobbs' in particular. All at once he spoke to me.

"Upon my word, Miss Thorn—I'm dreadfully sorry," he exclaimed—"but I believe I've been drinking your wine, I've been so busy talking, that I picked up the first glass I saw."

"That is my wine, Mr. Larrard," I said, pointing to a glass. Miss Dobbs had woke up, on hearing the raised voices.

"Then I have been drinking it," said Larrard, with a laugh. "Pray forgive me, Miss Thorn; this glass, which was meant for me, is untouched; won't you drink that?"

"No, thank you," I said.

"I'm more than sorry," he went on. "Really I shall feel that you won't forgive me, if you don't at least taste it."

"Drink it, my dear—drink it!" exclaimed Miss Dobbs. "Let's be friendly!"

They were both looking at me; I picked up the untouched glass, and drank a little; then, on Miss Dobbs laughingly insisting, I drank a little more. I absolutely refused, however, to finish the glass, and went off to bed, fully determined that nothing should make me sleep.

As a matter of fact, I was asleep in ten minutes, and I slept heavily. Something—some merciful Providence, I suppose—woke me while it was still dark; ashamed that I should have slept at all, I stumbled out of bed. My head was heavy, and ached horribly; yet I had some notion that there was something to be done—some need for watchfulness. I got to the door of my room, and opened it, and looked out. All was silent as the dead.

I was going back into my room, when a draught of cool night air fluttered my garments. Turning quickly, I saw that the great windows at the end of the corridor were wide open!

My brain was still whirling; yet I knew, dimly enough, that there lay the danger. Groping with my hands along the wall, to steady my shaking limbs, I got to the window; the cool air revived me, and slipping to my knees, I leaned out a little way. Down below, moving on the thick growth of ivy which covered the wall, I saw a figure clinging; someone was holding to the roots of the ivy, and climbing up. Even as I drew back in alarm, I heard a curious knocking, at the further end of the corridor, and then the startled cry of the child.

"Blades! Blades!—I'm afraid!"

The knocking continued; and I knew, in a dazed fashion, what was happening. Neal Larrard had disturbed the child—a thing easy enough, seeing that he was in the room adjoining. The knocking ceased; and then I heard the patter of childish feet, and the opening of a door. Another door opened, too, and the tall, white-clad figure of Larrard came out, and stood there.

Then the smaller figure of the boy appeared; stopped, on

seeing that still white form in the half-darkened corridor, and with a shriek of dismay, fled straight for the window. I had dropped down beside it; I managed, as the little figure came straight for that open space, to spring forward, and catch it in my arms. We fell together to the floor.

I have no very clear remembrance of what followed; I only set it down as it was photographed on my brain at the moment. I heard flying feet on the stairs above; I heard the voice of the woman Blades. She came straight on down the stairs, and into the corridor.

I was crouching, with the boy in my arms, down beside the window. The woman gained the corridor, and raced straight for the window, crying the child's name. She had almost reached it, when there rose up above it the face of Augustus Kealing— grim and horrible in that half light. Whether the man had climbed up to see what had caused the delay, or whether he had any intention of finishing the work himself, if the window failed, I know not. What I do know is that Blades, seeing him, stopped, and made a sort of blow at his face; the man swung his head back—seemed to miss his hold—and disappeared.

In that moment, I heard his shriek as he went down; heard the thud on the road below; and then—as it seemed, a long time afterwards—a heavy splash in the sea far beneath. I only know that I had hold of Blades, and that she and the little boy and I were all clinging together, and sobbing convulsively.

I left the boy and the woman, locked close in each other's arms, in the boy's room; I knew they were safe. And the next morning, before breakfast, Neal Larrard was gone; while, later in the day, a telegram to Miss Dobbs summoned me back to town.

But by that time the child had got over his fright of the night before; he parted from me tearfully. Blades said nothing; she dropped her taciturnity so far as to wring my hand, and to murmur something ridiculous about what I had done.

THE HAUNTED YACHT.

The more I thought about the matter, the more sure I was that I must sever my connection with the Secretarial Supply Syndicate. There was no blinking the fact that I was literally in a den of thieves and worse; more than that, I was being made an active agent in all they were doing.

I had time to think about it all, because, for a week or two, nothing happened. I went down to that innocent-looking place, the type-writing office, day after day, and listened to Master Bob Pilcher whistling popular tunes, very much out of key, the while he looked out of [the] window; or I read novels or wrote letters. Work there was none; Micawber-like,[1] I suppose we were waiting for "something to turn up."

Naturally enough, I talked about the matter to Philip Esdaile. I had given him a sort of promise, as you already know, that I would carry the matter through, and lay the gang (for whom I was innocently working) by the heels if possible. I wanted to be released from my bargain. I found Philip hard at work in his rooms—scribbling away as if for dear life. He stopped, and listened with a grave face, while I told him all that had happened, and what my objections were.

---

[1] Wilkins Micawber is an impecunious and feckless character in Charles Dickens's *David Copperfield* (1850) who, despite all evidence to the contrary, persists in imagining that "something will turn up" to save him and his large family from financial ruin and starvation.

"It's no good, Phil," I said, despairingly—"I can't go on. I'm only a weak woman, and the fight is too much for me. Let me off; let me get out of it, and forget that the Secretarial Supply Syndicate ever existed."

"All right, my dear," he said, with a sigh; and I was so miserable, that I did not even resent that term of endearment—"of course, you must do as you please. It's a pity—because it would have made such splendid copy; it would have meant a fortune to me. But, there—don't think about that; have done with it, by all means, and try something else."

I had had a sneaking hope that he might have put fresh courage into me, and urged me to go on; I'm afraid I thought of that comfortable three pounds every week; I'm afraid I dreaded going back to precarious things. However, it had to be done; I parted from Philip, and went off to see the manager, Mr. Neal Larrard. There I received another shock.

Before I had had time to overwhelm him with my resignation, he told me of what the next business in hand was, and what my part was to be. He began in quite a matter-of-fact fashion—a fashion which sent my heart into my boots; because I recognised that he felt sure, to begin with, that I was fully aware of what the business was, and what part I had to play in it.

"Miss Thorn," he said, on that first morning I had seen him for a week or two—"we start again to-morrow. This time, the business will require your most careful and devoted attention. Do you understand?"

He looked at me out of half-closed eyes, and I felt that I was beginning to tremble. We were in his private room, and I looked about me helplessly for a moment, before screwing my courage up to the point of telling him what I meant to do.

"Mr. Larrard," I said, in a low voice, without looking at him—"if you please, I'd rather not. I—I've heard of another appointment—and I'd like to take it." (I think the angels have forgiven me that lie, long since.)

"Indeed?" he said, coldly. "I may have a word to say about that. Are you dissatisfied with your position here—your salary?"

"I might—might do better," I gasped, beginning to see the hopelessness of my position.

"I see—it's a question of a rise in salary," he replied, with a laugh. "Well, Miss Thorn, your services are valuable; shall we say five pounds a week for the future?"

"I—I'd rather not," I replied. "I don't quite like the work."

His manner changed in a moment. Almost before I knew what had happened, he was between me and the door. His voice, when he spoke, was very low and very quiet; but it was also very deadly.

"I begin to understand; there is also something *you* must understand. You entered this business of your own free will—don't interrupt me, I beg. You have been associated with us in several affairs of a somewhat shady character; you are afraid to go on. Let me tell you that you *must* go on."

"Must?" I echoed, blankly.

"That was the word I used. Miss Thorn, believe me when I tell you that we shall not willingly place you in any danger; but you are mixed up in a business greater than you imagine. It is not myself only, or the men and women you have met already; this association, or business—call it what you will—has ramifications all over the world. In a word, we cannot allow anyone to leave us who knows anything of our secrets. You're quite young, Miss Thorn; why commit suicide so suddenly?"

I saw the dreadful meaning of what he said in his eyes; I had some evidence of the brutal nature of the man, in the fact that he strolled across to the writing table in the room, and carelessly pulled open a drawer in it; out of that drawer, apparently in the most careless fashion, he took a revolver, and examined it curiously—glancing from it to me with a strange smile on his face.

"You mustn't think you can threaten me, Mr. Larrard," I said, with more bravery than I felt.

"My child—I don't threaten you," he said, with a very unpleasant grin. "We never threaten; we act." He tossed the revolver back into the drawer, and shut the drawer with a bang. "Now then—how is it to be?"

I saw the hopelessness of it; I was silent. After a moment or two, he went on speaking, quite naturally.

"I want you to go to-day to Southampton," he said—"to take up your professional duties on the steam yacht *Mystic*. She lies there, in the harbour; she is going for a pleasure cruise—well—never mind where. I shall be on board; there may be other passengers. It will be a very pleasant trip, Miss Thorn—and will last about a month. A cabin has been reserved for you, and you will be treated with the greatest possible care and consideration."

"Am I to go to-day?" I asked, with a white face.

"This afternoon, if you please," he replied. "The train leaves Waterloo soon after three o'clock; travel by that, and go on board directly you reach Southampton. You are expected."

Like one in a dream, I took from him the money for my expenses, and made a brief note of his instructions. I telegraphed to my landlady that I was unexpectedly called away, and might not return for a week or two; she was to keep my room for me.

At the last moment, Mr. Larrard called me into his room, to give me final instructions.

"By the way, Miss Thorn," he said, "you need not take your typewriter with you; there is one on board. You will understand clearly that, in the event of any enquiries being made, you are simply engaged by the owner of the yacht, to act as his secretary during the voyage. You will remember that character, I am sure."

Remembering the title that I had heard bestowed upon me—that of the "Lamb"—I said demurely that I would remember; and so we parted. I had been so flustered at the idea of going off in that unexpected way, on some business I instinctively knew was connected with a fresh scheme on the part of the gang, that I had forgotten to make any preparations. I sent another telegram to my landlady, instructing her to put together certain articles I required, and to send them, in my portmanteau,[1] to Waterloo Station by special messenger that afternoon. At the last moment, also, I remembered that Philip would be anxious about me; I sent him a telegram, giving the name of the yacht, and some slight details concerning my movements.

I was in for it—that was certain. I may confess now that I was horribly frightened; I seemed to see this gang, of which Larrard was the chief, spreading its tentacles in all directions, and making it impossible for me to escape. My one hope was that I might be able, by great good luck, to bring them to justice.

A very nice and innocent-looking vessel the *Mystic* was, despite its name. Having no nautical knowledge, I cannot describe it; I only know that it was roomy and comfortable, and beautifully kept. I had myself taken on board, and was at once

---

[1] Leather trunk for clothes.

shown to a small deck cabin, very well fitted. I'm afraid I cheated myself into the belief that we might, after all, be relieving the tedium of business, by going on a pleasure trip somewhere or other. I was soon to be disabused of that idea.

I slept soundly that night in my small cabin—rather enjoying the new sensation than not. In the morning I went on deck, and the first person I saw was Mr. Neal Larrard, who smiled affably, and hoped I had slept well. I reassured him on that point, and asked where I was to work.

"I'll show you, Miss Thorn," he replied, and led the way below.

He unlocked the door of a cabin, right at the end of the vessel (you mustn't expect me to tell you which end, because I don't know) and introduced me into a neatly fitted sort of office. There, on a modest table, stood a typewriter; sheets of paper were lying about; everything, in fact, suggested the office I was to fill. I expressed some admiration for it, and some gratitude to him, for having given me such a pleasant place in which to work. He smiled; said I might care to look about me; and went on deck. A moment later, he came into the place, with a sort of rush and spring, and spoke rapidly.

"Sit down. Slip a sheet in. In God's name—move yourself! Now then, take down this!"

I knew that something had happened, although of course I had not the faintest idea what it was. In less time than it takes to write, Mr. Neal Larrard was lounging at the other side of the desk, with a cigar between his lips, and was carelessly turning over some papers. At the moment he began to dictate, the door was softly opened, and I saw, out of the tail of my eye, a small fair man, with a mere straight line for a mouth, gazing in upon us.

"We shall find, in all the great commercial undertakings

in the world, one guiding spirit," dictated Mr. Larrard, in his calm measured voice—"and one condition which makes for their success. Hullo!"—he called out, in apparent great surprise, as he raised his head—"what do you want?"

"Just having a look round, sir," said the small fair man, with a nod. "Without mentioning any names, you know me, and I know you. I am a detective-sergeant, and I hold a search warrant, which you may see if you like. We have our suspicions, sir, and I want to examine every inch of this remarkably well-arranged yacht."

"Examine it, and welcome," said Larrard, with a laugh. "You men are always making mistakes; I suppose I must put up with the inconvenience attending this one. May I introduce my secretary—Miss Thorn." I bowed stiffly. "You have interrupted us at rather an important point. I have to do a scientific paper, for a learned Institution; and have come on board here, for the sake of rest and quiet. Will you make your search, or whatever you call it (I don't in the least know what you want), and go away again?"

Mr. Neal Larrard spoke with so much of the air of one utterly bored by the proceedings, and utterly miserable at the idea of being disturbed, that I confess I was, for a moment, almost deceived myself. But the little man interested me very much; he seemed so much struck with my machine, and with the work I was doing.

While I sat there, quite still, with my hands just touching the keys, he seemed to pervade the place. His hands wandered about over the table, and he glanced sharply at me once or twice, and even took hold of the machine, and raised it up. And all the while those deadly eyes of Mr. Neal Larrard's were watching him covertly, and all the while one white hand of Mr. Neal Larrard was in the breast of his coat; and I knew what he was holding.

"Well—are you satisfied?" asked Larrard, with a slow drawl. "Or am I to be disturbed any longer?"

"Yes—I'm satisfied—for the present," said the little fair man. "When do you sail?"

"Haven't made up my mind," said Larrard. "Just as the whim takes me."

"There's a locked cabin next to this; what's in there?" asked the other, quickly.

"Oh—you can see, if you like," said Larrard, rising with a grunt. "It happens to be a steward of mine—drunken rascal I shut up there for safety, until he had slept off the effects of his bout. I didn't want him to set the vessel on fire."

He took his keys from his pocket, and sauntered out of the room, with the little man behind him. I heard him unlock that further door; and heard them both go in; heard whispering voices. Then the door was locked again, and they came back. The detective very politely took off his hat to me, as he was going. I was so frightened by the whole visit, that I felt he had my particular pattern of handcuffs jingling in his pocket.

"Good afternoon, Miss—Thorn," he said. "We might meet again, perhaps."

"I sincerely hope so," I responded, with a smile; and he was gone.

Mr. Neal Larrard very courteously escorted him to the companion ladder leading to the deck; I think he was even careful to see him go over the side. Then he came back to me. Coming into the cabin, where I still sat obediently at the machine, he dropped his hand on my shoulder, and laughed, and gave me a word of commendation.

"You never turned a hair," he said, giving me a little shake. "And what a squeak it was!"

"I don't understand," I began; and he laughed again.

"Of course you don't," he said—"how should you? My dear—you're a treasure!"

Of course by that time I knew that something was very wrong indeed; I trembled to think what unknown danger I might be associated with. For I knew that this man would, without the faintest compunction, drag me into any difficulty in which he might be, and declare that I was his willing accomplice.

At the suggestion of Mr. Larrard, I locked the office, and gave him the key. For the rest of the day, I had nothing to do; I filled in my time by wandering about the vessel, and examining and admiring all that I saw. The crew was not a very smart one, and no particular uniform was worn; however, they seemed to know their duties. About midnight, the throbbing of the engines warned me that we were starting on our unknown voyage; I was so deeply interested, that I went up on deck to see what was going on.

Now, I'm not a fanciful person, by any means; no one has ever accused me of that in all my life. Perhaps it might almost be said that I am, if anything, rather too practical and hard-headed for a woman. Therefore, I want you to take what I write now in no fanciful spirit; I want you to believe that what I saw and heard then, and what was afterwards explained to me, I really did see and hear; and that it had rather a startling effect at the time.

I had gone up on deck, just as the vessel began slowly

to move through the water. Of course, it was not a pleasant thing—even at the wonderful salary of three pounds per week[1]—for a young girl to be starting out for some unknown part of the globe, in the company of people of whom she had every right to be suspicious; so I suppose I felt rather melancholy, and perhaps a trifle sentimental. Be that as it may, while I leaned against the rail at the side of the vessel, and looked towards the receding shore with its many lights, I thought I heard near me a voice I knew.

It was utterly ridiculous; but it seemed to be the voice of Philip Esdaile. Several sailors were standing at a little distance from me, doing something with ropes and lanterns; and from the group of them there floated, as I thought, the voice of my lover (I think I may call him that by this time), singing a song we both had known, and had sung together, in happier times. I knew it could only be a fancy, born of the quietness of the night, and the stars, and my own loneliness; but it seemed very real. I turned, as the song ceased, or as I thought it ceased, and went below again.

Now, the worst of a yacht is, that one is so liable to lose one's way. In this particular instance, I forgot where my cabin was—failed to remember, in fact, that it was on the deck itself. Stumbling about down below, I came to the door of that cabin wherein I had sat, but a few hours before, at the typewriter.

The door was open a little way, and there was a light inside. Somewhat surprised, I drew nearer, with the intention of looking in; and, at the same moment, the door of the next cabin

---

[1] Both Bella and Larrard seem to forget his impetuous offer at the beginning of this episode to raise her weekly salary to five pounds.

opened, and a figure came out. Scarcely knowing why I did so, I got behind one of those things I believe are called bulkheads, and watched.

The man who came out from that cabin which had been locked—the man who was evidently the person described by Mr. Neal Larrard as his drunken steward—was one of the strangest-looking men I have ever seen. He had obviously wakened from a deep sleep; he was rubbing his eyes, and shuddering and shivering, like one not yet fully aroused. A young man, but yet with a curiously lined and haggard face, and with great dark staring eyes, that seemed to be looking all about him, as though in deadly fear. He stopped for a moment, and then went into the room in which the typewriter stood, and closed the door.

I confess I was puzzled. I did not understand why he should be in that room at all; but for the fear that I might get him into trouble, I should have gone to Mr. Neal Larrard, and explained that this drunken steward was in his private office. Instead of that, however, I waited and watched.

I think I have already said that these cabins were at one end of the ship; quite near to where I stood was a dark sort of cupboard, in which miscellaneous articles of all sorts appeared to be stored; the door was ajar, and I could only guess what was there, by the extraordinary mixed odours which came out of it. Hearing approaching footsteps, I slipped inside.

Peering out cautiously, I saw Mr. Neal Larrard coming along the narrow passage. After a moment's hesitation, he opened the door of that small office, and looked in; in deadly fear, and yet with much determination, I slipped out of my cupboard, and approached the door also. As Mr. Larrard went in, I stood within a yard or so of him, in that half-darkened little corridor;

and so was able to see all that went on inside, and to hear all that was said.

The first surprise I got was on looking into the room. Neal Larrard approached the table, where the haggard-faced man was standing, and, without a word to him, bent down, and seemed to move something at the side of it. Instantly I saw the typewriter slowly disappear backwards into the desk, as it were, while in its place came up a small machine, of quite another type. It had a sort of round plate at the top, so far as I remember; and it looked quite bright and new. The haggard-faced man bent over it, and began to move it about with his long thin hands, and to examine it closely.

"Now get to work," said Neal Larrard, roughly. "You've had your sleep out; and all your plates are ready. There's no fear of interruption here; we shall be miles out at sea in an hour or so, and you can work all night. I'll leave you to it."

"Let me break the accursed thing up," said the other man, passionately, making a movement towards the machine as he spoke. "I won't do it—I can't! I've been your tool too long already; any life—or any death—is better than this. I'll print no more of them!"

"Very well," said Larrard, with a contemptuous look at him. "We steam back into Southampton, and land you at once. The police are quite on the look out for us there; they searched the yacht this afternoon, while you were asleep. We'll give you up, Mr. Arthur Crane, for the murder of—"

"Stop—stop!" cried the other, in a hurried whisper. "You don't mean it; you'd never give me up like that. I'm sorry; I'll do what you wish—if there's no other way. Don't go back; you've been very good to me."

"Very well, then—get to work, and let's have no more of this," said Larrard. "You fool!—don't you know when you're well off? We'll make your fortune—and hide you at the same time. Get to work, I say. The plates are all right, I suppose?"

"I'll defy anyone to know the difference between the real and the sham," said the other, in a low voice, and with his head bent.

Watching eagerly, I saw the strange man pick up a sheet of thin flimsy paper. But that there was nothing printed upon it, I should have said that it was a bank-note; it had just that crisp rustling sound about it, when he spread it out on the machine. As he stood between me and the door, and as Larrard was shoulder to shoulder with him, I could not see what was done; only after a moment or two, the paper was held up, and I heard Larrard laugh.

"You're a clever rascal," he said, half in a voice of admiration. "Once get abroad, and we'll pass these things without the faintest difficulty. They don't ask questions on the Continent, if they see an English bank-note. I suppose," he added, "you can go on all night? You won't be disturbed. For safety, I'll lock you in, and leave you to it."

He moved towards the door, and I moved away. Regaining my cupboard, and stepping into it in the dark, I had an uneasy feeling that someone else was there; I certainly heard a rustling among the things behind me. The thought that it might be a rat was not a pleasant one; and I was glad when I heard Larrard turn the key in the lock of the office, and heard his retreating footsteps along the narrow corridor. The moment he had disappeared, I flew along to my room; examined myself closely, to be sure that there was no dust or dirt upon me; and then strolled on deck. We were out at sea, and not a light was to be seen.

After a moment or two, I went again to my cabin. I wondered what it all meant; I wondered particularly what I should do. Think of the situation: here was I, miles out at sea, and helpless; and yet actively engaged in screening a business at which I dared scarcely guess. Something told me that the best thing to do was to sleep, and hope that something might happen to guide me on the morrow.

I undressed, and got into my bunk. I could not sleep; I lay there, imagining all sorts of things, and seeing always that poor hidden ghost, working through the long night hours, in the locked room. I remembered that Larrard had accused him of murder; I supposed the man must be a criminal, hiding from justice. And just as I was in the middle of those thoughts, I heard a sound in the cabin.

It was a queer sound to hear in the dark, especially in such a place as that; for it was the sound of someone sobbing; very quietly, and in a hopeless, miserable fashion, as a child might do. But I was sure of it. Reaching out my hand along the wall, I touched the knob which would switch on the electric light; turned it down sharply, and sat up in bed.

"Now, then," I said—"come out, whoever you are!"

From under my bunk there crawled out a figure. It came out very slowly, and quite as slowly got on to its knees, and sat up there, with face buried in hands, sobbing more than ever. It was a boy.

Here was a pretty state of things! I had a sudden hot remembrance of the fact that I had undressed in that cabin, not half an hour before. I tumbled out of my bunk—hastily threw something round me—and dragged the boy to his feet.

"You young villain," I said, indignantly—"what are you doing here?"

"For God's sake—don't turn me out," was the boy's surprising reply. "I didn't mean any harm—only I couldn't stay there with the men, another night. I'm a woman!"

I sat down, and looked at the shrinking figure. It was a very pretty face that was revealed to me, when the hands were dropped from it; it was a very slight and delicate figure that was roughly hidden by the sailor clothes. Demanding an explanation, I got a startling one.

"I shipped on board," she whispered, standing quaking before me—"to follow the man I love. I have been near him, again and again, since he has been in danger. I cut off my hair, and shipped as a sort of steward. I was behind you in that cupboard just now, while you were watching him at work."

"I put you down for a rat," I said. "So you know this ghost—this man who stays hidden by day, and comes out at night, to work?"

"Yes," she said, looking round about her wildly—"I know him well. He was accused of a crime he never committed; he struck a man in anger, and believed that he had killed him. He was hidden away, by people he believed to be his friends—people who have since merely made use of him."

"In what way?" I asked, with a great suspicion growing in my mind.

"He is an engraver—one of the most skilful it is possible to find. Trading on his fears, and persuading him always that he was likely to be arrested for this supposed murder, these men have bent him to their will; this yacht has been taken only for that purpose; you are here only as a blind to cover all that is done. Now, while we're here, that poor hunted creature is printing forged bank-notes, which are to be distributed at the ports at which we call."

I looked blankly at her. "But what are we to do?" I asked.

"You're the only one who can do anything," she said, quickly. "You have access to that room, wherein the printing is now being carried on; you have to work there at your typewriter. If you could manage, by some means, to get the key of the room in which he is locked during each day, I could go to him; I could tell him what I know to be true."

"What is that?" I asked.

"That the man he was supposed to have killed is alive; that he has nothing to fear. He struck that man down, because the fellow had insulted me; I have brought all this trouble upon him. If only I can get that key, and get a chance to talk to him, I can get him away; and then, perhaps, we might manage to destroy those fearful things he is printing."

"Oh—you'd better leave that little job to me," I said, quietly. "I wouldn't like to think that I had no hand in the business at all."

We talked far into the night, the dawn was coming up over the sea when finally the girl crept out of my cabin, and ran on deck. By that time, I knew that her name was Olive Norton, and that she had simply added a letter to her Christian name, and had shipped as Oliver Norton. I had to hold myself in check that day, because I was really most wildly excited.

I had another shock, when I got on deck after breakfast. I was leaning on the taffrail,[1] when I heard again the refrain of the song I had heard the night before. Turning sharply, I saw a

---

[1] Rail around the stern of a ship.

sailor near me, coiling a rope. We happened to be alone on that part of the deck, and, without raising his head, he addressed me.

"Don't start or scream, or anything of that kind," said the voice of Philip Esdaile. "They were in such a mighty hurry to get off, when once they had you on board, that they shipped anybody, to make up the crew. I was hanging about, so they shipped me. I know all about the business—or I guess about it. I'm near, if you want me."

Still humming that refrain, the young journalist moved away; came back, a moment or two later, to add a word or two.

"It'll make such splendid copy!" he said; and went away again.

My responsibilities were increasing. To know that the man who loved me was on the yacht; to know that this tragic love story, between two young and helpless people, was also to be worked out there—all this was enough to turn anyone's brain. But I had to keep a clear head; and above all, I had to remember what must be done.

We made steadily, during the next three days, for the western coast of Spain. (This I only discovered afterwards; because, during those three days, I had other matters to attend to than those of navigation.) That poor creature, locked up all day in the cabin, had to be reached; I felt murderous, when I saw Mr. Neal Larrard walking about, and actually jingling his keys in his pocket.

On the third day, my opportunity came. We had seen land dimly all the afternoon; we were approaching port. That afternoon, Larrard came to me, and, to my utter astonishment, handed me the keys himself.

"Be busy in the office, if you please, Miss Thorn," he said. "We hope to run into harbour to-night, or early to-morrow morning; someone might come aboard." He grinned, and looked at me meaningly. I took the keys, as sedately as I could, and went below.

We dropped anchor that night, in the harbour of a little town on that northern coast of Spain. Some of the crew went ashore; I remained in the office below, pretending to work. Mr. Neal Larrard remained in his cabin, and, save for the solitary tramp of a sailor on deck, all was very still. I came out cautiously, and fitted one key after the other into the lock of the cabin wherein Arthur Crane was sleeping. Finding the right one at last, I noiselessly opened the door, and then gave the signal—a low hissing sound. The figure of the supposed boy darted forward out of the shadows, and slipped into the room.

I don't know what they said to each other; I have no notion of what broken words she used to persuade him. I only know that, in a moment or two, she came out with a new light in her eyes—and the poor ghost was with her. Without a word, he went to the table at which I had been seated, and pressed something at the side of it; the hidden printing machine came up. He took from it something that looked like stone slabs, walked to the port-hole, and dropped them into the sea. The girl gave a happy little laugh.

After that, the real excitement began. I know that, with another key on the bunch, I opened a safe, where, artfully hidden between letters and papers, I discovered all the forged notes that had been made; I had never held so much money in my life. I was reckless, and I thrust the whole mass on to the little fire in the cabin. They blazed up so fiercely, that some of them tumbled out on to the wooden floor; a new idea came to me. I turned to the girl.

"Take him to my cabin; lock yourselves in there," I said, in a whisper. "Don't answer, whoever knocks. When you hear an alarm raised, rush out, and get away in the boats with the others."

I saw them safely along the corridor and saw them go stealthily up the companion;[1] then, with my heart beating fiercely, I dragged out all the live coals from the little fire on to the wooden floor; saw them begin to smoulder, and then to burn into the woodwork; locked the door of that room, and of the cabin next to it; and took the keys back to Mr. Larrard. Then I slipped up on deck.

The rest is a mere whirlwind of terror and destruction. It was quite a long time before the flames were discovered; and by that time both cabins had burst out. In the noise and the confusion, while those of the crew who remained on board were rushing for the boats, Arthur Crane and the girl slipped in with the others, and were gone. I never saw them again, nor did anyone else connected with this story.

The yacht was doomed. It blazed fiercely all that night, while crowds on shore watched it, and gesticulated (as is the foreign manner) and made hopeless suggestions. Mr. Neal Larrard was good enough to congratulate me on my escape.

"I'm afraid one poor wretch has gone," he said; and I knew that he alluded to the ghost in the locked cabin. I smiled in the darkness, at the thought of how splendidly the retreat of that poor ghost had been arranged for.

Philip Esdaile contrived to get a whispered word with me that night. Mr. Larrard had arranged for a room for me at a

---

[1] Companion-way: staircase to cabin.

small hotel; Philip hung about in the street outside, until he saw me.

"Fine effect at the finish," he murmured. "I must keep out of the way—or they'd suspect me. But I'll keep a look out for you—of that you may be sure."

And, as a matter of fact, he travelled in the same train with us, unnoticed, when—a couple of days later—we started again for England.

THE SWINGLEY GREEN TRAGEDY.

At this distance of time, I forget how many weeks elapsed, before anything out of the ordinary happened at the office of the Secretarial Supply Syndicate, Limited. Now and then, it is true, I was sent out with my typewriter to houses and offices; but nothing came of it. Whether or not the gang was merely feeling its way, and failing, or whether it had occurred to Mr. Neal Larrard, the manager, that it might be well to make it appear that ours was a genuine typewriting office, doing legitimate business, it is impossible to say; I know I was relieved to find that, on more than one occasion, I did quite innocent work, and felt that I had fairly earned my money.

There came a day when Mr. Larrard received a visit from two men. One of those men I knew; it was the man known as Grimes, who had been prominent in regard to the attempted capture of President Penaluna, as related in my account of my first experience with the Syndicate. They were with Larrard, in his private room, for nearly two hours; all that I could hear was the low murmur of voices. When they came out—the three of them—into the room where I was seated, the conversation was being finished.

"Do you think you can manage to do it?" asked the man who was a stranger to me.

"Certain of it," said Larrard. "My dear boy—you won't know me. A Shakespeare collar,[1] and flat tie—hair a little oiled—I tell you you won't know me. I'll rub up my Latin a little—and I'll wear glasses."

"Steel rims!" ejaculated Grimes.

"Do you suppose I'd wear gold!" exclaimed Larrard, petulantly. "If I don't know how to fake the business by this time, you'd better give it to someone else. See that you do your part; see that I am the only one in the business."

Their voices fell down to mere whisperings; I heard no more. Presently, the two men left, and Larrard went back into his office. After about half-an-hour, he came out, and walked to the telephone; rang it, and asked for a number. I was apparently cleaning and oiling my machine; I listened intently, for something more than my mere womanly curiosity was aroused. I knew that we were on the eve of another scheme of some kind. When he spoke into the telephone, in a moment or two, his voice was entirely altered; it was mild and soft, and yet had in it a peculiarly earnest note.

"Are you Grand Hotel?" (There was a pause between each phrase I heard him use.) "I want to speak to Mr. Vincent Kendale—Only for a moment, if you please—Oh—he happens to be in the office?—Good morning, sir; are you Mr. Kendale?—Thank you; I must apologise for troubling you, but I heard, by the merest accident, that you were in town. This is the Secretarial Supply Syndicate—very well known—most highly respectable. I understand you want a tutor—Oh, no—nothing ordinary, by any means; between ourselves, we have supplied a

---

[1]   A pointed turn-down collar.

certain Royal personage with the same sort of thing—Exactly; I quite understand; the man must be a gentleman—Yes, I assure you he does; shoots well—rides well—everything you could desire—No—not at all; father a retired General; he came to me with strong recommendations from a very high quarter indeed—Thank you; he shall come to you this afternoon. Three o'clock?—Very good; at three o'clock Mr. Hawke will call upon you. Good-bye."

He turned the handle of the telephone, and walked away. As he moved across the room, I heard him mutter to himself—"Shan't want those Shakespeare collars, after all; quite another sort of character."

He went out soon after; and, when he came back, I positively rose from my desk, to greet him as a visitor; I did not know him. His hair, which, ordinarily speaking, he wore rather long, had been cropped close; the small moustache which usually just covered his upper lip was gone. His clothing was different; instead of the somewhat loose attire which had hitherto covered his great frame, he wore rather close-fitting tweeds, with a sporting sort of tie, and very neat leggings. He grinned, as he saw my astonishment, and swaggered forward into the room.

"Ah, Miss Thorn—it's better than I thought," he said. "Come now, would you set me down as a gay[1] fellow—who has run through his money—has a good education—and is willing to take up tutorial work, in a gentlemanly fashion, in order to live? Do I look the sort of man who would appeal to a young fellow, with plenty of money, who merely wants a companion, to help him kill time on his large estate?"

---

[1]   I.e. dissolute or licentious.

"I should think you would fit the part very well," I said.

"And you're not surprised at the change?" he asked.

"It is not my place to be surprised," I said, demurely.

He looked at me quizzically for a few moments, and then laughed, and walked through into his room. A little before three o'clock he came out; passed me with a serious nod, and strode across the room. At the door, he turned, and came back a pace or two.

"Keep the office open as usual each day. Should I telegraph for you, come at once, bringing the machine; close the office before leaving it."

At the end of the week a letter arrived at the office, addressed to me; it contained, folded within a half sheet of notepaper, three postal orders[1] for a sovereign each. Whatever his faults, I am bound to say that Mr. Neal Larrard always paid me promptly.

I used to send Bob Pilcher, the office boy, out on imaginary errands during those days—chiefly in order that I might get rid of him and his eternal whistling. One afternoon, at the beginning of the next week, when I was alone in the office, the telephone rang again, and I answered it. A voice I did not recognise in the least enquired if I was Miss Thorn; I replied that I was.

"You will go down at once—this afternoon—to Swingley Green, Norfolk. Take the typewriter with you; lock the office. Give the boy his wages up to the end of the week, and dismiss him. Are you clear?"

"No," I replied, sharply—"I am not at all clear. Who are you?"

"Never mind about that; suffice it that I have instructions

---

[1]   I.e. money orders.

from Mr. Larrard. There's a train leaves at three fifty-one from Liverpool Street; you will be met at Swingley Green, and will receive your instructions there."

"But who are you; how do I know—?"

"Good-bye," came the voice sharply, and the little bell under the telephone tinkled. I "rang off," and went back to my desk.

A sudden thought occurring to me, I took from my pocket one of the postal orders, which remained unchanged. In the little circle at the corner were the words "Swingley Green." I began to understand.

I never remember to have travelled in such a storm as there was that day. It blew hats about, and nearly overturned the cab in which I drove to Liverpool Street; it roared and buffetted and howled about the busy City;[1] and there were flaring posters out already, giving startling announcements of great gales and disasters on sea and land. When you add to that the fact that heavy rain came blustering with it, to flick across one's face like small whips, you may form some idea of my feelings, when I started on that unknown journey.

I got to Swingley Green in due course, and stepped out on to the desolate little wind-swept and rain-swept country platform. A melancholy-looking station master was bending his head to the wind, and vainly striving to make the guard understand something he was saying; a wet and disagreeable porter took my typewriter and small bag, and asked where I was going.

I said I did not know; and the man looked at me as though

---

[1] The business centre of London was referred to as "the City."

he wondered out of what particular lunatic asylum I had escaped. Just as we stood staring at each other, a big figure emerged from the little booking office—a figure I knew, even in its many wrappers, to be that of Mr. Neal Larrard. I was going to address him by name, when he took the words out of my mouth.

"You remember me—Mr. Hawke—don't you? You are Miss Thorn; and I have been sent to meet you. What a horrible night! Now then, porter, carry this lady's luggage out to the carriage."

A smart carriage and pair stood outside the station, its lamps gleaming in the darkness. Mr. Larrard (in that new character of Mr. Hawke) courteously handed me in; the door was slammed and we were off. I could not see his face in the darkness of the carriage; I had an indistinct feeling that he was very excited—much as a man might be at the crisis of some event towards which he has been working.

"First, Miss Thorn, as to your instructions," he said, in a low voice; and his hand gripped my arm closely, to bespeak my attention. "Of Mr. Larrard you know nothing; you know a certain Mr. Hawke—tutor and companion to a certain Mr. Vincent Kendale, who lives at the place to which we are driving—the Gable House, Swingley Green. Are you attending closely?"

"Yes," I replied, faintly, and heartily wishing myself back in London again.

"This young man—Mr. Vincent Kendale—has been a little wild in his youth; in consequence, his education has been much neglected; hence my presence here. For the rest, it has suddenly occurred to him—to *him*, you understand—that it may relieve him of trouble and anxiety, if he has a secretary who will—well—overlook his bills and accounts—write his letters, or type them; it is a whim, Miss Thorn; but it suits the purpose of that Mr. Neal Larrard who is not to be mentioned. Do you understand?"

"I understand," I said; "you have no need to impress upon me what my duties are."

"I felt sure of that," he said; and, although I could not see his face, I knew that he was grinning. "So that you see, quite naturally, I suggested that I would write to the manager of the Secretarial Supply Syndicate, and get them to send on someone reliable. So here you are. Now, having heard what Mr. Hawke, the tutor, has to say, I want you to listen next to Mr. Neal Larrard—who is practically non-existent."

His voice changed, and it was at once the dominant voice of the head of the gang I heard in the darkness of the carriage.

"Watch this man; watch his letters. I want to know everything about him; where he goes—what he does. You understand enough by this time to know what I mean; I need say nothing more."

I did not reply; if the truth must be told, I was desperately afraid. I was alone with this man, in a strange part of the country; I had already had evidence enough of his desperate character, and to what lengths he was prepared to go, in the carrying out of his schemes. My one plan, as it had been before, was, if possible, to frustrate whatever villainy Neal Larrard might be contemplating; I knew that open defiance of the man could only result in disaster all the way round.

I began to think that matters were very bad indeed, when I saw the face of the footman who opened the door; it was the man Grimes. However, I said nothing, and walked quietly behind the man to the room which was to be mine. I think he expected me to speak; if so, he had made a mistake, for once in his life at least.

Mr. Vincent Kendale, my new employer, sent a polite message to me, requesting my company at dinner that evening; dinner was to be served in half an hour. So I went down; and a very strange dinner party it was.

Knowing what I knew, I confess I sat there in terror. The young man—and he was very young indeed—had a kindly, good-natured, but rather weak face, and a pleasant voice and manner. He behaved to me in the most gentlemanly fashion, and informed me that he had arranged with his housekeeper to see to my comfort, and had had my room selected so that it might be next her own. He spoke always with a very perfect courtesy; but I think he took, during his dinner, rather more wine than was quite good for him. The only other person at table was the supposed Mr. Hawke, the tutor; and the only servant who waited was the man Grimes. Remembering my own unwilling connection with the gang, I thought that Mr. Vincent Kendale, had he but known it, was pretty well watched that evening.

I was puzzled to know what they meant to do. That the man into whose house they had forced themselves and me was enormously rich, I could guess; but I could not understand how they hoped to get out of him any of his money. I did not know what excuse they would use, nor what method.

He was such a good-looking fellow, and had behaved in such a kindly, gentlemanly fashion to me, that I burned with indignation, to think that these fellows were plotting against him. I wanted to rush out, and tell someone; in the silence of that great house at night, the dread of what they might do almost overpowered me. I could not sleep; I did not even make any attempt to undress.

My room was in the oldest part of the house—or so I judged it to be; and it was within a few feet of the ground, as I discovered on opening my window and looking out. The storm had abated; only a little drizzle of rain was left. The night, I remember, was very still—very still indeed, by comparison with what it had been on my journey. Knowing well that I should not sleep, and feeling grateful for the soft fresh country air on my face—so different from that air I had breathed at the window of my attic in London for so many months—I turned out my light, and knelt on the floor by the window, and looked out into the dark grounds.

The night was so dark, that there was no possibility of my being seen from outside. When, presently, I heard a stealthy footstep on the path just below me, I remained perfectly still, with my eyes just on a level with the window ledge. Then I heard a soft scratching sound, and saw a dimly defined figure, upright, with arm raised as if in the act of throwing something. I knew that the stealthy visitor, whoever it was, had picked up some gravel, and was throwing it at a window. The next moment I heard a little rattle just above me; some of the gravel dropped down past me.

Directly after that, there came swift steps across the room above; then the window above was opened, and I heard a quick whisper.

"Hist! she's down below here," came the voice of Larrard from above.

"Who?" asked the voice of someone below me—a voice I knew.

"The Lamb," answered Larrard. "He arranged for her to sleep there. Is the light out?"

"No sign of a light anywhere," said the voice again from beneath me. "Can you come down? I have news."

"I'll come at once," replied Larrard; and I heard his window close.

I remained where I was. I knew they could not reach my window from outside, because it was just above their heads, and the ground below it, I felt sure from the position of the figure I had seen, dropped away rather steeply. I knew, too, that I could not be seen; and the absence of light would make them suppose that I had already retired.

I heard a door opened near me, and a bigger figure stepped out, and joined the first. Dimly I saw the two grip hands; then I heard a name I remembered.

"Well, Whittaker—and what's your news?" asked the voice of Larrard.

I remembered at once that Whittaker had been the name of the elegant and well-dressed young man, who had figured so prominently in the theft of the diamonds of La Belle Obrino.

"I think it's all arranged," said the voice of Percy Whittaker. "The insurances are settled; those notes, supposed to be signed by this Mr. Vincent Kendale, in which he expressed his willingness that you should insure his life, in order to protect you from loss for the sums he owes you, were quite effective. I've arranged it with five different offices; and in five different names; under each of those names, you draw the amounts after his—"

"After his death?" supplemented Larrard, quickly. "Good; you've managed the thing very well. Now, there's another business on hand—a matter which concerns you. It will suit you; it is a little matter of love."

"That, certainly, is more in my line," said Mr. Whittaker, with a laugh. I held my breath to listen.

"This young fool here is in love with a girl—supposed to be the richest in the county. Her father's estate joins this; the old fellow objects to the match—won't hear of it—because this Vincent Kendale has been wild and reckless; he wants someone more settled for his daughter. So they're going to elope."

"Well—I can't see how that concerns me," said Whittaker, after a momentary pause.

"It concerns you in this way; that we get, in this case, a sort of double deal. This young fool is got out of the way, and we secure the insurances. That leaves the girl; and you'll elope with her."

"That's cool—'pon my word!" exclaimed the other.

"The fellow Kendale," went on Larrard, "has given me his confidence in everything. He is to elope with the girl at night; I know every detail of the plan. The night he elopes—or is supposed to elope—will be the night of the accident; you understand what I mean? The girl will wait; you will take Kendale's place by her side, and go off with her."

"But the object?"

"The object is, that her father is a very wealthy man, and will do anything to avoid a scandal. She elopes with you—ex-forger—ex-thief—ex-valet—and is hopelessly compromised. Her real lover is dead—or will be, by that time; you have taken his place. That ought to be worth something, to hush up a matter of that sort. If you come to that, you might go so far as to marry the girl, and then secure the lot. In any case, the blackmail ought to be good."

"I rather like this part of the business," said Whittaker, with a disagreeable laugh. "I'm going down to the inn; walk with me a little way, and tell me what I am to do. By Jove, Larrard—I see myself in this part!"

They moved away out of hearing, and I knelt there for a long time, wondering what I was to do. This man, in whose house I was, was to be done to death; the girl he loved was to be made the unconscious victim of this scoundrel. I tried to think, but could not; and I suppose at last, from sheer weariness, I must have fallen asleep.

I awoke some hours later, and closed the window; then, without undressing, I lay down on the bed, and slept again, uneasily enough. With the morning, I felt more calm and composed; my brain was actively at work to devise some means of helping Mr. Vincent Kendale and the girl.

I had nothing to guide me, because I did not even know for what time or day the elopement was planned; I could only watch. And, in turn, I may say that I, too, was watched.

If Mr. Neal Larrard was not by any chance in the room wherein I sat as secretary to Mr. Kendale, then Grimes contrived to be there. Even if I seemed, for a moment, to be alone with the young man, while he dictated a few business letters in a haphazard fashion, I always knew that outside the partially opened door one or other of them was at hand. If, by any chance, I managed to screw my courage to the point of speaking, either Larrard or Grimes came into the room, on some pretext. And at last, during the afternoon, when I had grown quite desperate, Larrard seated himself at a desk on the further side of the room, and remained there. Then it was that an idea occurred to me.

Mr. Vincent Kendale had grown weary of the business of dictating, as he seemed to grow weary of most things; he sat idly beside the machine, looking at the mechanism of it, and lazily touching a lever here and there. Quite carelessly, I made a suggestion.

"Wouldn't you like to know how to type?" I asked; and, out of the corner of my eye, I saw Larrard look up quickly. Evidently feeling, however, that I was merely trying to interest the young man, he smiled, and turned again to what he was doing.

"Is it easy?" asked Mr. Kendale. "It's pretty work, at any rate; yes—I'll have a shot at it."

I made way for him, and stood beside him at the table, with my back towards Larrard. Mr. Kendale began laboriously to type out a word or two—swearing softly to himself, I fear, when he happened to hit the wrong key. After a moment or two, seeing that Larrard was unsuspicious, I bent over, and put my hands on the keys, and spoke quickly and brightly.

"Let me show you," I said. "Now, watch me carefully."

Very rapidly, while I stood beside him, I typed out the words—*"You are in grave danger; I want to help you, and the girl you love. Before God, I mean what I write."*

I tilted back the carriage of the machine, and laughed, and pointed to it.[1] "What do you think of that?" I asked; and I'm afraid there was a little tremble in my voice.

He bent forward to read; started suddenly, and looked round at me. I saw the expression of his face change, while I looked

---

[1] Early models of the typewriter were "blind"—i.e. the type bars hit the underside of the roller so that the typist could not see what she or he was typing. The text was visible only when the carriage was lifted. Machines with typing that was visible to the operator were available by 1900, but Bella appears to be using an older model here.

steadily at him; then he caught hold of the paper, and suddenly whipped it out of the machine.

"That's all right," he said, as he tore the paper up into small pieces, and walked across to the fireplace. Dropping them into the flames, he came back again; and I saw him glance at Larrard. "Now I'll try," he said—"and you shall put in words after mine. We'll see who does it best. Jolly game—isn't it?"

"Very," I said, demurely.

"I hope you two are amusing yourselves over there," said Larrard from his end of the room, with a laugh. "Is he an apt pupil, Miss Thorn?"

"Seems to understand everything at once," I said; and I saw a grim smile flicker across the face of Mr. Vincent Kendale. He began to type slowly again.

During the next five minutes, Mr. Vincent Kendale laboriously typed out some very vital questions; I rapidly answered them in the same fashion. As the questions and answers grew more exciting, he laughed once or twice, in a boyish fashion, like one looking forward to a fight, and rather enjoying the prospect. We had filled a page, and were intent upon our work, when I heard a movement at the other side of the room; Larrard had risen. I'm afraid I was guilty of the great rudeness of driving my knee into Mr. Kendale's side, as a species of hurried warning.

"I want to see what the new typist is doing," said Larrard, strolling toward us.

In a moment my pupil had whipped the paper out of the machine, and had crushed it up in his hand. "No—there are too many blunders," he said. Then he shouldered Larrard aside, and went to the fire, and dropped the crumpled paper in; stirred it well down into the flames with the poker. But by that time I knew what to do, and where to meet him that night.

By a strange freak of Fate, Neal Larrard himself gave me a free hand. Late that evening he came to me, and told me that the next day was to be my last at the Gable House. "I've made all arrangements with Mr. Kendale," he said, "and you can return to town; you will be wanted at the office. You have served our purpose very well," he added, in a lower tone; "you have given an unsuspicious appearance to things."

I wondered then how much my life would be worth, if Mr. Neal Larrard knew the part I had played. Quite smilingly, I thanked him for his good opinion of me, and bade him good-night.

I knelt at my open window for a long time that night, until I heard steps below me, and a quick light whistle as of a bird—the signal I had agreed upon with Mr. Kendale. Then, as he moved away into the darkness, I climbed on to the window-sill, and let myself drop. It was only a few feet, but the ground sloped; and I came down, in a very undignified fashion, on hands and knees. I was rather glad Mr. Kendale had walked ahead.

I came up with him—still following the note of that strange bird—in a shrubbery at some distance from the house. There I told him the whole story; of the gang with which I was innocently associated; of the plot I had overheard; and of what they meant to do. His rage and horror, when he heard of the plot against the girl, was frightful; it was with difficulty I calmed him.

"You will do no good by violence," I said. "I know these men; and I know that you would endanger my life, as well as your own, if you did anything but meet them on their own ground. You must plot against them in return. I am supposed to leave here to-morrow—doubtless in order to get me out of the way. Instead of that, I intend to go to the station, and then to return here; I will be at the place you have arranged to meet this lady; I may be of assistance. Understand, however, that I must get out of the way as soon as I have seen to your safety, or else they may suspect me."

He wrung my hand, and thanked me again and again. "This shall be a lesson to me, Miss Thorn," he said. "I honestly believe you've saved my life; I'll do something better with that life, in the time to come."

"Give the best of it to the woman you love," I said; and he told me, with tears in his eyes, that he would.

Now, it is all very well to promise a thing; it is quite another matter to carry it out. Here was I, a weak girl, ignominiously dismissed to London, and yet with all the weight of this business upon me, and the knowledge that I had to save a man's life and a woman's honour. And yet, through it all, I had to keep a calm, quiet face, and go about my work like a machine.

The plan we had arranged was this: the carriage which was to take Vincent Kendale and the girl away that night was to be in the road, outside the grounds, an hour earlier than had been decided upon before; this, in order to frustrate Larrard's plans. There was a deep lake at the end of the grounds, near to the road in which the carriage was to wait; I shuddered when I thought to what purpose that lake was to be put. On the other hand, I did not mean to go away from Swingley Green, until I had seen that all was well with the young couple.

Accordingly, when the time arrived that I must take my departure for London, I was driven, in some state and ceremony to the station, accompanied by my typewriter and my modest bag. Mr. Vincent Kendale ceremoniously saw me off from the house, and thanked me for my services. But we knew that we should meet an hour or two later.

Arriving at the station, I sent the carriage back again, and had my belongings put in the cloak room. Then, by a circuitous route, I made my way back to the grounds of the Gable House.

It was not a very dignified position; but I lay in a shrubbery for over an hour, with all sorts of unpleasant things crawling over me, waiting for the coming of the lovers. Heaven knows then I had no idea of the tragedy in which I was to figure; I acted in all simplicity. But for the fact that a woman mistook the time, and was late, there need have been no tragedy at all.

I must explain that, knowing I must get away, after the departure of the lovers, as rapidly as possible, I had arranged with a fly-driver[1] at the station at Swingley Green to be outside the grounds of the house, in the same lane from which the lovers were to start, at nine o'clock that night; if I could not actually manage to get away from the little town itself, I felt that I could at least put up at an inn, and return to London in the morning.

After a long and weary wait I heard that bird whistle again, and saw Mr. Vincent Kendale coming through the darkness. He dropped down beside me, and we conferred in whispers.

"It's all right," he said. "I shall never be able to thank you, or to repay you. You were absolutely correct in what you imagined. A suit of my clothes—one in which I most ordinarily appear—has gone; and Grimes is the man who looks after my wardrobe."

---

[1]   A fly was a small, single-horse carriage, often—as here—for hire.

"Then Mr. Percy Whittaker will appear to-night in the character of Mr. Vincent Kendale," I said, laughing.

"And will find the two birds flown," he replied.

We waited for a long time; Mr. Kendale more than once stole out, to see if the girl had arrived. Once he managed to get a glimpse at his watch, by means of a match; it was long past the time. Waiting anxiously and impatiently, we became aware of two or three figures moving silently on the margin of the lake which stretched before us; Vincent Kendale pointed them out to me.

"They mean business," he said. "Good Heavens!—where should I have been this night but for you?"

I had arranged, as I have said, for my own conveyance, and had given particular instructions as to where it was to wait. Mr. Kendale, creeping out for the last time, hurried back to me with the information that the girl was there, and was in the carriage, and that my own humble fly was waiting also. Giving him a moment or two in which to gain the carriage and get away, I had the satisfaction of hearing the noise of the wheels, and the flying hoofs, as he went off down the road.

I had to think of myself; I knew the men about me. I made a dash through the shrubbery to the spot at which I knew the fly was waiting; and, as I did so, I heard hurrying footsteps coming after me. I gained the door of the fly, panting and breathless, and pulled it open. As I got in, a man sprang in after me. I leant out of the window, to call to the driver, and heard an exclamation from the man beside me, who had seized my arm.

"God!—it's the Lamb!"

I knew the voice; it was that of the man Whittaker. Before I had time to speak, he had scrambled out of the fly, and was making back towards the lake. In the semi-dark-ness, and with those clothes which had belonged to Vincent Kendale on him, I could have sworn it was Vincent Kend-ale himself. And then, while I watched him, scarcely know-ing what to do, there came, in a moment, the tragedy.

Three or four figures seemed to spring up suddenly out of the ground, as it were, and to close about him. He cried out something, and tried to beat them off; I heard the sickening sound of blows; and then, while they all struggled together, there was a splash, and the waters of the lake were troubled and broken up; then the shadows of the men were racing for dear life across the grounds. I knew what had happened; they had taken Percy Whittaker, in his disguise, for the man they had come out to kill.

I got away in the fly to the station; told some absurd story about the necessity for getting back to London; and prevailed on the station master to stop a lumbering goods-train.[1] On that I got away, and got back to London; arriving—cold and hungry, and horribly frightened—at about four o'clock in the morning.

---

[1] Freight-train.

THE MUMMY.

I had a good many points to consider, before returning to the office of the Secretarial Supply Syndicate, and facing Mr. Neal Larrard. As time had gone on, each business in which I had been concerned with them had grown more desperate; remembering that last tragedy at Swingley Green, and the dead man who lay at the bottom of the lake, I was afraid to think what was to happen in the future.

On the other hand, when I came to think about the matter as calmly as was possible, it occurred to me that they could not, under any circumstances, suspect me of having any knowledge of the business. For all that they knew, the body of young Vincent Kendale was at the bottom of the lake, and Mr. Percy Whittaker was gone with the girl; it was only afterwards that I knew that, on applying for the insurance for the former, they discovered that he was alive, and that their plot had failed. As to the death of Percy Whittaker, they must have guessed at that.

Knowing that I had—as they supposed—got away to London before the tragedy, it occurred to me that I might with safety resume my duties; indeed, if I did not, the probability was that they would suspect that I knew more than was good for me to know. So the next morning—a little hollow-eyed and very nervous—I resumed my seat in the office of the Syndicate.

For obvious reasons, I heard nothing concerning my last adventure; indeed, for a few days I was left alone in the office. When at last Mr. Neal Larrard came back, I saw that he watched me anxiously, as though he would have liked to know how much I knew concerning that business of Swingley Green; he dropped an occasional hint or question, as to my journey back to London, and what train I had caught, and so forth. I gave him minute information, and apparently satisfied him.

But for that former threat of his, and my fear of what would happen if I severed my connection with the office, I should undoubtedly have made some excuse to get away; above all, the boy Bob Pilcher was gone, and I was alone in their hands. It was, therefore, with much satisfaction that I heard, on the very day of Mr. Neal Larrard's return, that I was to go away to a new client on the outskirts of London. Greatly to my satisfaction also, the new business appeared to be quite of an innocent character; I thought it possible that I was going in order to fill up time, or to allay any suspicions which might have got abroad concerning the Secretarial Supply Syndicate.

"I want you to go to-morrow, Miss Thorn, to Barnet," said Larrard, after calling me into his private room. I saw that he was watching me keenly while he spoke, but I felt that that was only due to the fact that he was suspicious of me at that time. "A certain Professor Corder-Smith—a very noted scientist—is in want of a secretary, and has been recommended to us. Your duties will be very pleasant; the old gentleman is writing a series of articles on some abstruse subject, and requires a typist to write from his dictation. As it is rather a long way away, and as the Professor has a bad habit of working late at night, you will be provided with a room in the house. The Professor's sister will look after you, and you will, I think, have rather a good time of it."

Mr. Neal Larrard smiled enigmatically as he spoke, and I thanked him for having made such thoughtful arrangements on my behalf.

"You will go down to-morrow morning, Miss Thorn, and will, of course, take your machine with you. I cannot say how long you may have to remain there; these scientific men are somewhat erratic; in any case, you will receive due notice as to when you should return."

"Are there any special instructions, Mr. Larrard?" I asked.

"Well—the Professor is rather particular in his habits, and he does not like any prying or poking about amongst his treasures. Rummy old chap; he has all sorts of queer things from all parts of the world; don't be frightened at anything you see—will you?"

"I am not easily frightened, Mr. Larrard," I said, smiling at him demurely. He grunted, and his face hardened a little as he looked at me in return.

"I don't think you are," he said.

I went down next day to Barnet, having first packed a small bag, and made arrangements with my landlady to keep my room in readiness for my return at any time. As a matter of fact, I was rather looking forward to this new excursion; I saw myself doing interesting work, in the house of a man of culture; above all, I saw myself, for a time, out of the hands of the gang with whom I had been associated. So, quite light-heartedly, I took the machine, and went down to Barnet.

I had quite a long drive, after leaving the station; and when at last the four-wheeler drew up at a gate in a high wall, I began to wonder what sort of man this was, who lived so far out of London, and in such a dreary-looking spot as this. In response to my tug at the bell, an old man came shuffling out to the door, and opened it, and admitted me. The door was closed behind me, and I heard the cab rumble away; then, without a word, the old man (who looked like some servant who had grown elderly in long service) led the way across a neglected garden, staggering a little under the weight of the machine.

I have never at any time been so astonished as I was when I entered that house. Outside was the neglected garden, cumbered with weeds, and utterly untended; inside, the house was a palace. Rare and wonderful embroideries and tapestries were strewn about, like so much lumber; curious gold and silver ornaments, studded with precious stones, actually littered the tables, and even the floors; packing-cases, crammed with rare things from all parts of the world, were in every room in the house. As I am a living woman, the mirror in the room assigned to me as a sleeping apartment had once reflected the face of Marie Antoinette, and must have been worth more than I dared think. I felt very small indeed, with my humble typewriter (so curiously out of place, in that house stuffed with old-fashioned things), and I wondered a little what my employer would be like.

The room into which I was shewn was the most wonderful of all, so far as its treasures were concerned; and in the midst of all the treasures sat an old, old man—the owner of everything there.

He greeted me with a gentle courtesy, and explained what he wanted me to do. His sight had failed him, and no optician had been able to render him any permanent assistance. Although almost at the end of his days, he had still much to do, in regard to a great life work which was to hand down his name to an admiring posterity; he wanted to dictate to me that which he found it impossible any longer to write. He had approached the Syndicate, and they had unhesitatingly recommended me for the post.

He struck a silver gong which stood on the table beside him, and the old man who had admitted me came in. The Professor requested that Miss Corder-Smith might be summoned; and a few minutes later an old lady came in. I was introduced to her, and given into her care.

For nearly a week I led a very happy life. The work was very light; all I had to do was to type from the Professor's dictation for about two hours a day. More work than that exhausted him; so that I was free, for the rest of the time, to wander about the rooms, and to look at everything contained there.

The Professor evidently knew the value of what was in the place, for the fastenings of the doors and windows were tremendously strong. Every window was shuttered with solid steel, so arranged as to be easily moved by means of levers from the inside, but impregnable from outside. The bolts and bars were absolutely those of a prison; I remember that I laughed at the thought of how impossible it was even for Mr. Larrard or his friends to gain an entry.

Of course I was always haunted with the idea that some plot was afoot, in which I was once again to play an innocent accomplice; yet I could not see any indications of any movement on the part of the gang. I had a kindly note from Mr. Neal Larrard, enclosing my salary for the week, and trusting that I was quite comfortable; but that was all. For the first few days I lay awake at night, thinking that I heard noises in the house, or the forcing of a door or shutter; all was still as the grave. I came to the conclusion at last that I had simply been sent to this place out of the way, and that Mr. Larrard and his friends were unaware of the wealth scattered about in the lonely house.

There were two other servants beside the old man who had admitted me—a stout comfortable couple, who had evidently been attached to the household for some time. The wife acted as cook, and the man, who was her husband, was a sort of elderly footman. The old man to whom I have referred had practically nothing to do except to answer bells (which were very rarely rung) and to sleep away the greater part of the day in a little room at the end of the hall.

Near the end of the week, the Professor came into his study one morning, in a state of great excitement. He held a letter in his hand, and he was chuckling softly to himself as he read it.

"A great day this, Miss Thorn—a very great day indeed," he said. "The dream of my life is fulfilled; the very key to all that I have been working at so long is to be supplied to me."

I expressed my curiosity, and the Professor, seating himself beside my table, proceeded to enlarge upon the subject.

"As you are aware, Miss Thorn, from the work we have been doing these past few days, I have all my life been studying that most fascinating subject, which still lies beyond our ken, I fear—Black Magic. That is to say, I do not, of course, as a cultured man, believe in any of these things myself; I am merely constructing a history of superstition—the black art—ancient and modern astrology—everything, in fact, which lies outside the merely practical."

"A very interesting subject," I said.

"Interesting—and vast," said the Professor. "I have not yet decided into how many volumes the work will extend; it may take years, if I am spared to finish it. But this that is coming to-day opens a new door for me, as it were; or at least I hope so."

"May I ask what it is?" I enquired.

"It is a mummy," said the Professor, in a sort of awed whisper. "Not an ordinary mummy, by any means," he added; "they can be bought for the proverbial song. This mummy has cost me thousands; I have had to bribe, here, and there, and everywhere; to charter a special expedition, in fact, in order to secure it. It is no other than the mummy of the great and justly celebrated Amra Ka, of—I forget the exact date B.C.—first and greatest of all astrologers—one to whom every secret concerning the stars and the universe generally was supposed to have been revealed."

"But how will this mummy help you?" I asked.

"There are believed to be certain writings upon the inside of the sarcophagus which holds the mummy; more than that, certain of his writings are believed to have been buried with him—perhaps even wrapped about him when he was originally put away. The mummy of Amra Ka arrives to-night."[1]

There were several other mummies in the house; some standing up grimly in corners, and others lying locked away out of sight. I confess I was a little bit interested myself in this particular mummy, because I suppose the mysterious always appeals to anyone of us; I wondered how much the Professor believed in the occult character of his long-dead guest.

---

[1] Nineteenth-century British and European interest in Egyptology had been sparked by Napoleon's expedition to the Nile in 1798, which included scientists and archeologists, and by the subsequent discovery of the Rosetta Stone in 1799. A fragment of ancient text was inscribed on the Rosetta Stone in three scripts—hieroglyphics, Egyptian demotic (a simplified version of hieroglyphics), and ancient Greek. The presence of the Greek text enabled scholars to decipher ancient Egyptian hieroglyphics, which they had previously been unable to decode.

I went to bed that night, and tried to sleep. As a matter of fact, I was a little bit disturbed in my mind, because I had seen the mummy brought into the house that evening by the railway men; and it had so much the appearance, in the semi-darkness, of a coffin, that I didn't like to think of it lying down there in the darkness; all the dreadful mysteries and secrets of that far-off time seemed to be hovering about it, and I must own I shivered in my bed, and felt I should be glad when daylight came.

I suppose you understand that curious fascination which seems to draw one to anything that is absolutely repellant. Struggle against it as I might, that dreadful mummy drew me like a magnet; I strove to dismiss it from my mind, and to think of something more pleasant; but still it drew me. If all the stories concerning it had been true, and it had possessed in death the power it once had had in life, its power over me could not have been more strong.

Incredible as it may appear, I rose at last from my bed, and put on my dressing-gown, and went down towards the study. I turned back twice in the silent house; but it was no use; I simply had to go down, if only to see that the dreadful thing was still in the place in which I had seen it deposited.

It was a ghostly house by night; it was so crowded with strange and weird things, that they seemed absolutely to start out at one from corners everywhere. As I went down, I stumbled against the pedestal of an Indian idol, the grim face of which gleamed wickedly at me, in the faint light which came from a staircase window; I drew away from it, with a little smothered shriek, and ran down a few steps, before I quite recovered my nerve. But for that idol, I think I should have gone back again; but I did not care to pass it.

I heard all sorts of creakings and rattlings as I went down through the house; more than that, I was almost convinced that I heard a stealthy movement in the study itself. However, I set my teeth, and got to the door of the room, and pressed myself against it, listening. With one desperate effort, I turned the handle, and went in.

A long stream of moonlight came from a high window, and fell across the room. Curiously enough, it seemed to single out the mummy-case above everything else; the long coffin-like thing, with its rounded head, gleamed as if with an unnatural light. I stole into the room, to have a closer look at it.

I don't know whether or not Mr. Amra Ka had been famous for his beauty, in his old Egyptian days, or not; I should think decidedly not. What was supposed to be a rough representation of him was cut into the lid of the sarcophagus; and a very moon-eyed sort of face it was that smiled up at me. While I stood looking at it gingerly, I saw to my astonishment that the lid of the thing had been shifted, and lay a little over towards one side; in the space between the sarcophagus itself and the lid I could see some grey wrapping material inside.

I cannot account for it; but I was filled with an unconquerable desire to see what Amra Ka looked like. I shifted the lid, so that it slipped over on one side to the floor, and peered in.[1] Instead of seeing, as I had anticipated, the tightly-bound mummy, I saw instead that the wrappings were loose; the face and head were hidden, and only the body and legs had any semblance of shape about them.

---

[1]   Gallon seems to be misinformed about the nature of ancient Egyptian sarcophagi, which, being made of stone, would not have lids that could be moved around as easily as the one on Amra Ka's sarcophagus.

While I was staring down at the mummy a very curious thing happened. I thought at first it might be the effect of the moonlight; but that light was too steady and unwavering for that. What happened was this: that the grey wrappings heaved ever so slightly, as though the dreadful thing inside them were breathing!

I got away in a great hurry; fascinated, I knelt on the floor at the other side of the room, and heartily wished myself back again in my own room. Then, while I watched, the thing in the sarcophagus began to stir; the wrappings were tossed and flung aside, and Amra Ka slowly and cautiously raised himself up, and looked about him; then, in a very undignified fashion, he sneezed twice softly.

By that time I had got over my fright; dreadful as it had seemed at first, in that silent moonlit room, it ceased to be dreadful when the thing sneezed; that took away from it, in a moment, whatever of horror it might otherwise have possessed. I knelt there in the semi-darkness, watching it; and I saw it sit up, quite leisurely, and shake the wrappings from it, and turn its face round to the moonlight. And I knew the face.

Not Amra Ka—ancient magician and astrologer; but Mr. Neal Larrard—most modern and up-to-date of rogues. It was fortunate for him that the sarcophagus was a large one; for it must have been a tight fit for him to get in. Evidently, too, he had been rather warm there, for he fanned himself vigorously with a corner of the grey wrappings as he looked about him.

He looked so funny, sitting up there, that I laughed; that has always been my undoing, that the ridiculous appeals to me. Hearing the laugh, he first of all dropped back into the sarcophagus, and then, raising himself carefully, looked over the edge of it in my direction. I rose to my feet, nodded at him quietly, and walked across the room.

He was more disconcerted than I ever remember to have seen him. Finally, however, after a long look at me, and observing that I appeared to be quite undisturbed, he laughed in turn; and asked me, in the most natural fashion, how I was. I assured him of my good health, and enquired if he was comfortable.

"You take things coolly," he said, in a whisper. "Is there anything in this wide world that could astonish you?"

"I think so," I replied, "although I don't quite know what it is."

"Now," he said, "to business. I don't know why you come spying down here to-night—"

"I wanted to see the mummy of Amra Ka," I said quietly.

"The mummy of Amra Ka no longer exists," said Larrard, with a quiet laugh. "He was in the way; we broke him up, in the hope that they might have stuffed him with something valuable. Now, listen to me. Go back to your room; remember nothing that you have seen; hear nothing during the night."

I began to see what all this meant. I saw that helpless old man, alone in this room, at the mercy of the thing he had brought into it. I saw Neal Larrard actually in the stronghold, able to admit anyone he pleased; in terror, I seemed to imagine any number of men swarming over the place—overpowering the few servants—and stripping it of its treasures.

"How did you manage it?" I asked; and perhaps I conveyed into my voice some suggestion of admiration at his daring.

"We had heard for a long time about the Professor; we could find no way to manage the business. Then came the mummy, about which the scientific world was talking. One of our friends was actually on the expedition; others joined the service of the railway company that brought the dear old astrologer here to-night. In the van, the change was made; the great Amra Ka, in several pieces, rests behind a dead wall, about a mile away from here. We drilled some air holes, and I, having everything ready, got in. Hush—I hear someone moving in the house. Go back to your room. Stop a minute," he whispered, as I was going, "pull this lid on first."

I saw that he had made up his mind that I would willingly keep silence; I felt that he thought I would not betray him. As he lay down again, with one final grin at me, I pulled the lid back into its place, and glided out of the room.

I wondered what I should do. Of course, I had fully made up my mind, if possible, to try conclusions with this new Amra Ka; yet I wondered how I was to set about it. To warn the old Professor, and send him down to the room where Neal Larrard lay in wait for him, would be simple madness; as a matter of fact, I did not know whether Neal Larrard might not have managed already to admit some of the gang to the house. I got back into my bedroom, and tried to think.

I heard someone moving in the house. That seemed to confirm my worst fears, and I own with shame that I was afraid to open my door to look out. I went to the window, with some vague idea that I might be able to see someone who would help me; instead, I saw in the bright moonlight which flooded the neglected garden three figures moving stealthily—in fact, I was just in time to see the last figure drop from the top of the wall into the grounds. Then, while I waited there irresolute, I heard cautious footsteps going along the corridor outside my room.

I am glad to say then that I plucked up courage to act. I

opened my door quietly, and looked out into the corridor; at the far end of it, I saw a figure going along, with a candle held above its head to light its steps. No midnight burglar this, but the venerable figure of the Professor himself. And he was going straight down towards the study.

Remembering what he was to meet there, I followed him. I made no noise as I glided along the corridor; I was careful, of course, to keep out of the way, and to take every advantage of the shadows, in order that he might not discover me. I wondered whether I had disturbed him, or whether he had heard anyone else moving about. I think that at that time I had quite made up my mind that I would save him from Mr. Neal Larrard, if I possibly could, at whatever risk to myself.

He entered the study. Setting down his candlestick on the table, he stood looking at the mummy-case with a satisfied smile, rubbing his hands, and gazing at it with the air of one who looks upon the greatest treasure of his life. By that time I was actually in the room, but had managed to glide behind a long hanging tapestry which shielded me from view. While I stood there, I heard the Professor talking to himself.

"That sister of mine was afraid I should not sleep if I tackled Amra Ka to-night," he muttered, with a soft little laugh. "She didn't understand that I shouldn't sleep at all until I had dipped into the mystery. Now, if only she has not heard me, I may yet have a chance to find out if the old fellow really— "

My dread was that he should move the lid of the sarcophagus; I held my breath while he went near to it. To my satisfaction, however, it seemed that he only desired to deal with the outside of the lid; there were certain signs and marks upon it, which evidently excited him greatly, and which he could read as easily as I could read my own language. While he knelt beside it (little suspecting, poor gentleman, what lay hidden inside), I heard him muttering to himself in a tongue I did not know.

"My theory is evidently right," he said. "This man desired that his final rest should not be disturbed; and so resolved to work upon the fears of the ignorant, in order to prevent his tomb from being rifled. If I were not a scientific man, and superior to such superstitious ideas, I should feel a little quaking at the thought of disturbing him. This is really very interesting; he threatens the gravest disaster—even death itself—to the man who shall disturb his final rest. I think I will translate this first, before proceeding to examine the interior of the sarcophagus."

The Professor, after another attentive reading of the lid, sat down at his desk, and began to write. Owing to his failing sight, his face was very close to the paper; he scribbled away at a great rate; evidently fearful of forgetting what he was writing, or what he had read. Gradually, however, while he wrote, tired nature asserted itself; his head drooped forward more and more, until finally the pen dropped from his fingers; and, with his head lowered on the paper, he slept.

The silence in the room grew oppressive—but I dared not move. With only the light of the candle there, and the faint moonlight streaming in from outside, I saw the lid of the sarcophagus slowly raised; saw the evil face of Neal Larrard peering out into the room. In a moment or two, the lid was slipped noiselessly on one side, and Larrard raised himself in the coffin-like thing, and looked out. Then, still with the grey clothes wrapped about him, he got out, and moved softly across the room.

I wonder I did not cry out, as I saw him bending over the sleeping man. Apparently satisfied, however, that the sleep was a heavy one, Larrard made for the door—almost brushing against me, where I stood drawn up close against the wall behind the tapestry. I heard the faint rustle he made, as he slipped out of the room; I guessed that he was going to let in his accomplices; and yet I could do nothing. I had just made a half-hearted movement to go and rouse the sleeping man, when Larrard crept back hurriedly into the room. He was a weird object, with those grey wrappings about him; he stood still, quite near to me, while he muttered impatiently to himself.

"I wish I'd followed my first idea, and trusted the Lamb," he muttered, little thinking how closely I stood, almost beside him. "I never quite know what to make of that girl; yet I might have got her to secure the keys. I can do nothing without them; I must get them somehow—if I have to choke the old man first."

A shrill whistle sounded from the garden—an impatient whistle, which told me that the men there were tired of waiting. Larrard made a movement towards the sleeper, and I made a movement also, scarcely knowing what I did. I drew back again, however, on observing that Larrard crept past the Professor, and made for the window. Keeping his eyes on the sleeping man, he fumbled at the levers and bolts of the shutters, until he had managed to get them free; then he drew the shutters open, and peered out. I saw him wave an arm down towards the garden, as a sort of signal, and then come back into the room.

The Professor was waking slowly—moving with quaint grunts and sighs, and much blinking of his eyelids. Just as he slowly raised his head from the table, I saw Larrard stripping off the grey wrappings from his head and shoulders, and making towards him. It was impossible for the Professor, even had he been wide-awake, to see him; Larrard was just behind where the old man sat. Then it was that I suddenly sprang into action.

I don't know what gave me the idea; perhaps it was the fact that I was wandering in a strange house, at that hour of the night, when I should have been in bed. At all events, I suddenly thrust aside the tapestry which concealed me, and stepped out into the room. Keeping my eyes closed, I advanced with a solemn step towards the old man. And I may assure you, incidentally, that it required some courage to do so, with the knowledge that Mr. Neal Larrard was looking straight at me.

He gave a sort of gasp, and cried out; I still advanced steadily. Opening my eyes the least little bit, I got a glimpse of the Professor starting to his feet, and looking at me in astonishment; then he suddenly moved towards me, and laid one hand on my arm. That was my cue; I opened my eyes wide—gave a startled exclamation—and began to scream for all I was worth.

I had no idea that I could scream so well. I suppose I added a little to my natural powers in that direction, by the fact that I was highly wrought up at the moment, and literally on the verge of hysteria. I have an indistinct recollection now of seeing the Professor swing round, and face Larrard; of hearing doors opening above, and people running downstairs; of seeing Larrard flinging his wrappings from him, and making a rush for the window. Then, quite forgetting my part, I fainted in dead earnest, and went down with a very unpleasant thump on the floor.

I remember coming to myself in that room, with the kindly arms of Miss Corder-Smith, the Professor's sister, about me, and with the Professor himself, looking deeply concerned and troubled, bending over me. The two men-servants and the cook were there, looking very much alarmed, and the window at the end of the room was wide open.

"It's the most extraordinary circumstance I have ever encountered," said the Professor. "If I were superstitious, I should really believe that the mummy of Amra Ka had come to life again, and taken itself off, by aid of that black magic he practised in life—to some other region; being a practical man, I can only believe that some scoundrels, envying me the great and wonderful discovery I have made, have endeavoured to steal my treasure from me. Fortunately for me, however, they cannot have gone far; I shall yet be able to recover the mummy."

"The mummy?" I said, faintly.

"My dear Miss Thorn," said the Professor, "you will be astonished to hear that this house has actually been invaded, in some extraordinary fashion, and the mummy of the great Amra Ka carried off. See—the sarcophagus is empty."

"I suppose, Professor," I said, innocently, "that that must have been what woke me. I never knew myself to do such a thing before—to walk in my sleep like that."

"Very extraordinary," said the Professor. "You must have been thinking too much about the mummy."

"A great deal too much, I'm afraid," I said, with a shudder.

I never saw the Professor after that time, because I left that queer old house at Barnet the next day; but, though he has advertised far and wide, he has never discovered Amra Ka; and he does not know how narrow an escape he had that night, when, for the first and only time, I walked in my sleep.

THE RETURN OF MR. MAGGS.

My position, after that adventure in the house of Professor Corder-Smith, was a very different one from what it had been before. For the first time, I had taken an active part in opposing Mr. Neal Larrard and those who worked with him; I had to make some explanation, and the question in my mind was whether or not that explanation would be received as a true one. I feared that, by this time, they had grown perhaps a little suspicious concerning "the Lamb," and I was dreadfully afraid of what might happen when I had to face them again.

More than all that, I came to know that I was being shadowed. It happened that the day after my return from Barnet was a Sunday; and I took quite an innocent walk, in order to compose my mind a little, and perhaps with the faint hope that I might meet that rising young journalist, Mr. Philip Esdaile. As it happened, I did meet him (he had once casually informed me that he sometimes walked in that particular direction on a Sunday morning), and I noticed that he looked particularly grave when I told him something of the happenings of the past week or two.

"I can't see what the end of it's to be," he said. "Don't you see, my dear Bella, that you are hopelessly involved with this gang; there seems to be no way out of it. I know perfectly well how many lines such men throw out, in various directions; unless it can happen that the whole gang is captured, and the evidence against them overwhelming, you must always go in fear of what may happen to you. On the other hand, they may actually drag you into the business, and swear that you have been actively engaged in their villainies."

"Don't you worry about me, Phil," I said, a little sadly—"I daresay I shall manage to take care of myself. I don't mind admitting I'd like to be out of it all, and to have finished for ever with the whole business; but, as you say, I must wait until the end. I've got to go back to the office of the 'Secretarial Supply Syndicate, Limited,' and I've got to put the best face I can on the matter; in fact, to use an American phrase, I've got to 'bluff' the thing through. They dare not kill me; and I think they've got to be civil to me," I added, grimly. "You see, Phil—I know such a lot about their little tricks."

"Bella," he said, slipping his hand under my arm—"will you promise that if you manage to get safely out of their hands, you'll marry me? I want to help you to get away from all this sort of work; I want to work for you myself. You see, I'm doing very well just now, and I think we could manage together, with a little economy—eh?"

"Yes—," I said, quietly—"if I get out of their hands, I think I'll ask you to look after me for the future." But, although I said it lightly enough, I felt that the business was rather a hopeless one. I did not know then how soon I was to escape.

It was after Philip Esdaile had left me that I realised I was being followed. When I first came away, on that Sunday morning, from the house wherein I lodged, I had seen a grey-haired, quiet-looking man, neatly dressed, lighting his pipe on the other side of the road; he had given me a quick glance as I passed him. And now again, as Philip left me at the corner of the street, this same man was once again applying a match to his pipe, and eyeing me quietly over the bowl of it. In order to be quite sure whether or not the man really meant to watch me, I did not go straight home, but took a route which led me a mile or so round. And I had the uneasy feeling always that the man was dogging my footsteps.

Coming at last to the street in which I lived, I entered the house without once looking round; but from behind the curtains at my window, I looked out, and saw the grey-haired man on the opposite side of the street. So that altogether I passed an uncomfortable Sunday.

When Mr. Neal Larrard came to the office the next morning, he found me busily engaged cleaning and oiling my machine, ready for work. He stopped for a moment, and I felt he was looking at me; I merely wished him "Good-morning," demurely, and went on with my task. He grunted something in reply, and went through into his office. I felt that he paused there for a moment, at the door of the room, and looked back at me before entering.

A few minutes later, he sauntered out into the office. If I had expected him to speak to me about that strange adventure with the mummy I was destined to be disappointed; he merely paced up and down the room for some time without speaking. Perhaps even then I had the curious feeling that this man, despite his villainies, had behaved well towards me, and that I had done but little in reality to earn my salary. Be that as it may, some impulse prompted me, while I bent over my machine, to speak to him.

"Mr. Larrard," I began, timidly.

He stopped in his walk, and faced round upon me. "Well," he asked—"what is it?"

"I am being watched," I said, in a low voice, and with a glance at the door; and I then proceeded to tell him about the grey-haired man with the pipe on the previous day.

"I know—I know," he said, impatiently. "Everything seems coming to a head; we are being beaten at every point; failure after failure has come upon us. We used to be lucky enough—but lately—you are not going to betray us?" he added, suspiciously.

"I do not understand you," I said, gravely. "I have merely desired to warn you."

"If I thought you meant anything else," he said, looking at me with a scowl, "I would have but small mercy on you." And he went into his room again, slamming the door after him.

For two days I sat in that office, doing nothing. Occasionally the telephone bell rang, and Neal Larrard attended to it; on such occasions, the few curt words he said in reply to some message or other conveyed nothing to my mind. On the third day, however, the telephone rang again, while he was in the outer room; he went to it. For a few moments, I saw his head bent, while he listened intently; then gradually his face lit up, and he grew more and more excited.

"In London?" I heard him say. Then he went on speaking excitedly, and pausing sometimes for the reply. "Secure him by any means; get him here, if you can." There was another pause, and he went on again, after listening. "He'll have them about him somewhere—that's certain. Get him here; leave the rest to me."

For some little time after that, he was in and out between my room and his own, in a great state of excitement; he did not seem to know how to keep still. Presently he went out, and I was left alone in the place again.

I was to receive visitors that day. Mr. Neal Larrard had not been gone five minutes, when, looking towards the outer door of the offices, I became aware that it was being cautiously opened. Inch by inch it moved, while I sat staring; and when it was wide enough open to admit a head, a head came round it. It was that of the grey-haired man, who had followed me so persistently on the previous Sunday. Seeing me watching him, he nodded quickly, drew himself completely into the room, and closed the door again.

"Well—what do you want?" I asked.

"Now, don't you get upset, Miss," he said soothingly, as he came near to where I sat. "I know you're not concerned in the business, and I'm not going to mix you up in it, if I can help it. I'm looking for a man named Maggs."

"I have not the pleasure of his acquaintance," I said, drily—"and I don't think you'll find him here."

"I think I shall," he said. "He was concerned in a certain diamond robbery."

I remembered then that supposed amateur author, who had made off with the diamonds which had been stolen and hidden in my machine; I remembered that his name was Maggs. I said nothing, however, but merely looked at the little grey-haired man, as if expecting him to go on.

"As a matter of fact, Miss, I am connected with Scotland Yard;[1] and I've been watching you for a day or two. I know you have nothing to do with the matter, but you were once employed by this man Maggs, at the time those diamonds were

---

[1] The elite detective unit of the London Metropolitan Police was known as Scotland Yard, so named because the rear entrance of the unit's original headquarters opened onto Great Scotland Yard.

lost. Since then, he has been trying to get rid of them—has even succeeded, in one or two instances. He's been in hiding in London for the past day or two; that was why I kept a watch on you. I believe he'll be coming here to-day; and I mean to lay hands on him."

"I'd advise you to bring someone with you," I replied—"you may have an ugly lot to meet."

He nodded curtly. "I thought as much," he said—"I'm obliged to you. And I promise you I won't get you into trouble, if I can avoid it." He nodded again, and glided out of the room as noiselessly as he had entered.

Mr. Neal Larrard came back soon after, and casually enquired if anyone had called; without looking at him, I shook my head, feeling desperately ashamed of myself as I did so.

During the afternoon, several people did call. In quite a casual way various men strolled in, and went into the inner room, where Larrard was waiting. I saw two faces I had seen there before—and pretty villainous faces they were; I saw Mr. Grimes, who had assisted at one or two of my adventures, and who grinned familiarly as he came in. By the time the last had entered, there were five men in that inner room, in addition to Mr. Neal Larrard. And they seemed to be waiting for something, or for someone.

It was growing dark, and I was thinking about getting a light, although I had nothing to do, when the door opened once more, and the last figure crept in. A moment after, the figure—that of a man—went to the door again, and peered anxiously along the corridor outside; then came back into the room, closing the door carefully. There was something familiar in the face, although at the same time I did not remember to have met the man before.

"Larrard in?" asked the man, in a quick whisper.

"I—I'm not quite sure," I replied, looking at him closely. It had needed but the sound of his voice to convince me who it was. This was the white-haired, elderly man who had once dictated to me some lines of that novel which was destined never to be finished. The white hair was gone, as were other parts of his disguise; but I knew that this was the man Maggs, so eagerly expected, and so anxiously awaited.

"What do you mean?" he asked, coming a little nearer towards my table.

"I mean," I replied in a whisper, without moving, "that it will be better for you to slip out of that door again, and to give this office a wide berth. You are wanted rather particularly, Mr. Maggs—and I—"

I saw him move away from me towards the door, looking at me with a startled face; then, at a sound behind me, he stopped abruptly, and looked over my head. At the same moment, I heard the voice of Larrard, and knew that he had quietly entered the room from his own office.

"So here you are," said Larrard, in a suppressed voice. "Welcome back to England, Daniel Maggs; shall we say that bygones shall be bygones?"

"You're very good," said Maggs, with rather a sickly grin. "I've made rather a mistake, I know—but I—"

"Most people do make mistakes, when they turn against their best friends," said Larrard, with a little comforting laugh. "However, my boy—don't let's think of that; the blunder is done with. Just step in, and let us talk comfortably."

I was horribly frightened, although I kept as quiet and apparently as cool as usual. I got up from my desk, to move round it, with the sole object of facing Neal Larrard. I saw him standing there, holding the door, and waving a hand towards the inner room. Daniel Maggs, after a moment's hesitation, stepped in. Immediately afterwards, I heard a quick cry of surprise, and knew that the man realized he had been trapped. Larrard's big bulk filled the doorway, and I heard him laugh, before he turned the handle again, and closed the door—thus shutting himself and Maggs into that inner room with the others. Then there broke out a very babel of voices.

Within the next few minutes, I did some very hard thinking. I realised that Daniel Maggs was wanted very badly by Scotland Yard; I knew also that the men who had trapped him in that inner room knew nothing of that fact, and had simply called him there in order to have a reckoning with regard to the stolen diamonds—perhaps I should say, the twice-stolen diamonds. Here at last seemed to be my chance; here was the whole gang—or, at least, the more important members—gathered together in one place, and unsuspicious of danger. Think of what I had to face.

I was the human buffer between the forces of law and order, and that desperate band of criminals in the inner room. More than that, I was placed in the unfortunate position of not knowing when the grey-haired man, with the support I had cautioned him to provide, would arrive—or, in fact, what might happen before he did arrive. I crept to the door of that inner room, and knelt down by it, and put my ear against the keyhole. They were not cautious what they said, and made no attempt to moderate their voices. I heard everything.

It was Maggs who was speaking. From the sound of the voice, I should imagine that he had his back against the wall at one side of the room, and was literally at bay.

"I tell you I know nothing about them," he said. "Curse the things—they've been my ruin! I never had a chance from the first; they seemed to spot me, as a likely one to have them, especially as I had been seen with that typewriter of yours, who came to me from the man most concerned in the robbery—the valet, Percy Whittaker."

"Where are the diamonds?" asked the voice of Larrard. "Cut the patter; where are the stones?"

"I—I don't know," said the other, sullenly; and a sort of roar seemed to break out all round him in a moment. "It's no use making a fuss about it; it's the fortune of war," he went on, hurriedly. "I was robbed in turn; someone discovered I had the things about me, and I was half murdered for the sake of them. I lost the lot; I've been wandering the earth like a beggar these past few weeks—poorer than I ever was before. Come, now—you said it was to be a question of letting bygones be bygones; I've made a blunder—let's forget it."

"We can't afford to," said the voice of Larrard again. "Our very existence depends on the fact that each one of us is loyal to the rest. You thought it wise to take matters into your own hands; to rob us all of what was the common property of the band. You shall have one last chance—and one chance only."

There was a death-like silence for a moment; and then the voice of Daniel Maggs spoke.

"Well—what is it?"

"Give up the diamonds—every single stone of them—and forfeit your own share—and bygones shall be bygones. Come—the diamonds!"

"I tell you I haven't got them," began Maggs again; but

he said no more than that. I heard moving feet, and once the voice of Larrard directing the others to do something; I could not catch what he said. I thought I heard once a sort of cry— and then, above the noise of the struggle going on within the room, the voice of Daniel Maggs rose again.

"Let me go! By God—if I get out of this alive—"

The struggle was renewed more fiercely than before; I knelt there, trembling and shaking from head to foot—dazed and frightened—and wondering what I should do. Then I heard the voice of Larrard speaking in very low tones, and evidently giving instructions. I crept back to my desk, and sat there.

The door of the inner room was opened, and Mr. Neal Larrard came out alone. I noticed, as he came and rested one hand on the side of my desk, that the hand was trembling, and that he had to hold the side of the desk tightly, in order to keep himself from swaying about. It was quite a moment or two before he was able to speak.

"You are a wise girl, Miss Thorn—and know how to be quiet—and say nothing. We—we are closing the office to-day—"

"Yes?" I said, in a dull voice.

"There—there has been an accident. It doesn't concern you"—he laughed in an odd way—"and it's nothing important. Only we shall not require your services again. Do you understand?"

I bowed my head slowly; I wondered what had happened. Above all I wondered how they had managed to silence Daniel Maggs, and whether they really had got the diamonds from him. More than all, perhaps, I was so horribly frightened that my chief desire at that time was to get out of the place; to let the little grey-haired man from Scotland Yard fight his own battles, and make his own arrests; and to have done with the whole business for ever.

Mr. Neal Larrard quite quietly put his hand into his pocket, and drew out my week's salary. Although the week had only just begun, I knew that I was entitled to it, strictly speaking, although I hated myself for taking it. But I knew that I should only rouse suspicion in his mind if I refused. So I took it, and thanked him, and began to put on my hat and my coat. He did not say a word all the time, but simply watched me quietly. When I had finished, he held out his hand to me and spoke:

"Good-bye, Miss Thorn," he said. "You are perhaps the strangest girl I ever met; I'm quite sorry to part with you. Don't make enquiries about me, please; I shall, in all probability, go abroad to-night; at all events, this place knows me no more. Once more, thank you—and good-bye!"

I took his hand, and then prepared to go. I saw him still watching me as I went out of the door; I think I closed that door with a feeling of relief. I was again cast on the world—but it was a clean sort of world, after all.

I was destined not to get away so easily. Half way down the stairs, someone stepped out from a dark doorway, and confronted me; it was the little man with the grey hair.

"I've been looking about for some time, Miss," he said. "What has happened?"

"I haven't the least idea," I replied. "All that I am anxious about, at the present time, is to get away. Your man Maggs is there—and several other people also. If you want them, you had better get your men together, and go back. I've done with it all."

He caught me suddenly by the arm. "Not so fast, if you please, Miss," he said. "We want you; you know too much about the business for us to let you go like that. Come now, be sensible; go back again."

"Never!" I ejaculated, trying to break away from him.

"Now, it's no good, Miss; you will only get yourself into trouble, quite needlessly, unless you do what I tell you. Go back again—any excuse will do—and wait until I come. I tell you all the men are here; we expected a fight of it, and everything is ready. No one shall harm you, I promise you. Go back."

I went back. The door I had hoped never to open again opened at my touch, and I went in. As I did so, Larrard came hurrying out from the inner room.

"Hullo—what's wrong?" he asked.

"I—I've forgotten something," I began, lamely; and was surprised to find that my voice was a mere whisper. He looked at me quickly, and then cried out. At the same time, I heard a quick whistle from the inner room, and the doorway was filled in a moment by three or four excited figures.

"Police!—three or four of them just come in down below," whispered one man.

"I saw 'em from the window," corroborated a second. "Who's given the thing away?"

I saw Larrard look at me; then, without a word, he strode across to the outer door, and turned the key in it. "Catch hold of her," he said, in a low voice; "stop her mouth if she calls out. Sharp there; we haven't a moment."

Two of the men seized me, and turned me with my face to the wall. Larrard and the others went into that inner room; and, while I stood there trembling, I heard them dragging something across the floor. As they stumbled hurriedly through the communicating doorway, I turned my head, and looked at what they were doing.

The dreadful thing they were dragging between them across the floor had once been Daniel Maggs. I caught one hurried horrified glimpse of the swollen distorted face; and then, with a shudder, turned away my head. When I looked again, I could not help crying out, although my cry was an inarticulate one.

The desk at which I usually sat was a large one, and had a hollow space underneath, into which my legs were put while I sat at work. Into this space they were cramming the body of the dead man—wedging it in tightly, by main force. While they did so, and while the two men held me securely, I heard a sudden twisting of the handle of the outer door, and then a heavy knocking.

"Bring her here—quick!" cried Larrard, in a sharp whisper; and the two men twisted me round, and marched me towards the desk.

I saw what they meant to do, and I struggled with all my might. "No—no—for God's sake!" I cried. "I won't do it; let me go!"

They spoke no word, and I was, of course, helpless in their hands. They forced me down into the chair in which I usually sat, and literally lifted me—chair and all—until my knees were thrust far under the desk, so as to hide what was hidden there. I felt the horrible thing actually pressing against my legs.

While they held me, and while I begged and prayed that they would let me go, and swore that I would not betray them; and while the knocking on the door outside still sounded heavily, Neal Larrard darted into his room, and came back carrying something in his hand. He sat down quickly beside me, and I felt him press something hard against my side.

"Now, then—be reasonable," he cried, in a fierce whisper. "This is the last chance, and I don't mean to be sold by you. Move, and I pull the trigger, and face the music afterwards. Quick—your hands on the keys; write!"

One of the other men had slipped to the door, and softly turned the key; as the door was thrust open, I heard, as in a dream, the voice of Neal Larrard—calm and cool as ever—dictating to me; mechanically, my fingers touched the keys, and I began to type. While I did so, I felt that fearful dead thing pressing against my knees, and felt also the muzzle of the revolver hard against my side.

I haven't the faintest notion of what I wrote; I know that I heard his voice quite close to me; I know that there was a tumult in the room, and that the little grey-haired man was the first of a small party that burst in. Neal Larrard looked up indignantly; the men who had been in the room with him from the first were lounging about, moodily staring out of the window, or idly watching me as I worked.

"Really—really—you mustn't disturb people in this way," said Larrard, with a drawl. "What on earth do you want?"

"You know well enough what we want," said the little man. "You have a man Maggs here—Daniel Maggs—out on license.[1] He is suspected of the theft of certain diamonds, and I hold a warrant for his arrest. You are hiding him—but I mean to have him."

"I haven't the least notion of what you are talking about,"

---

[1]   I.e. out on parole.

said Larrard. "If you will have the goodness to look at that inscription on the door, you will see that this is a typewriting office, and that we have our own respectable business to attend to. Pray go away. Now then, Miss Thorn—attend to your work."

"Miss Thorn," said the little grey-haired man, "I charge you, in the King's name,[1] to assist us in this case. The man Maggs is here, and I mean to have him. Do you know where he is?"

I felt the revolver pressed a little harder against my side; half fainting, I slowly shook my head. I saw the little man look troubled; he spoke a quick word to two of his men, and they fell back to guard the outer door. Then he came further into the room, and opened the door of the inner office.

"You seem to be taking a great deal of trouble, my friend," said Larrard; but his face was white. "Pray search the premises, if you care to do so; only don't disturb my work."

He went on dictating, while the little man went quickly into the inner room, and looked about him. After a moment or two he came out, looking more puzzled than ever, and turned quickly to me.

"Miss Thorn," he said—"I have your word for it that this man Maggs is in this place. I've had my men posted, and I know that he can't have escaped. He's in the rooms somewhere; I call upon you to say where he is."

I looked up at him; I opened my mouth to speak. Mr. Neal Larrard shifted a little, and the revolver muzzle absolutely hurt me.

"I—I know nothing about it," I said, faintly. "It—it was a mistake."

---

[1] I.e. King Edward VII, Queen Victoria's eldest son, who reigned from 1901 to 1910.

The little man held a whispered consultation with two of his men, and then moved reluctantly towards the door. I saw his men slowly moving with him; I saw my last chance and my last hope going. I knew that I was an accomplice, indeed, this time, and that I was assisting to hide the crime that had been committed. The little man with the grey hair actually had his hand on the handle of the door, and was passing out, when my chance came.

I had sat so still, and I suppose my answers had been so satisfactory, that Mr. Neal Larrard, for a moment, had his suspicions disarmed; I felt the revolver had dropped away from my side. In a moment, as it seemed, I cried out, and started to my feet; flung out one arm, which caught Neal Larrard squarely across the face, and tossed him backwards; and with the full weight of my body overturned the desk on which the typewriter rested. I heard a loud report, and felt a sudden fierce pain in my left arm; saw the hideous doubled-up thing against which my knees had rested roll out on to the floor; heard a great tumult in the room. Then, while men seemed to be fighting and struggling all over the place, everything appeared in a moment to vibrate about me, and the walls to shake and tremble as if stirred by a wind; and I fell heavily to the floor.

•   •   •   •   •   •   •   •   •   •   •   •   •   •   •   •   •

Never since that day have my fingers rested on the keys of a typewriter; I feel I could not do it. Not that there is any great necessity; because that young journalist, Mr. Philip Esdaile, who has a quite mistaken notion that I possess virtues no one else has discovered, has insisted on earning a joint living for himself and me for some years past; in other words, I am Mrs. Philip Esdaile.

The only echo of my connection with the office of the Secretarial Supply Syndicate, Limited, comes to me from a newspaper cutting—(one of many)—which I have treasured. It relates to the trial of Mr. Neal Larrard and his accomplices—a trial upon the details of which I need not enlarge, as it has long since passed into criminal history. Here it is, and with it I will end the chronicle of my adventures:—

"Perhaps the most remarkable feature of this trial, and certainly the most remarkable of the many witnesses who gave evidence against the prisoners, was this Miss Bella Thorn. Slight and girlish, and said to be but little beyond her teens, she stood hour after hour in the witness-box, in the crowded court, with her arm in a sling, and gave in a quiet, cool, matter-of-fact voice those damning details, which proved how closely she had studied the methods of the gang. She appeared quite unmoved by all that went on about her, although dire threats were uttered more than once against her by the desperate men she accused. She was quite unmoved also, so far as appearances went, by the commendatory remarks of the Judge, and by his congratulations to her on having escaped so cleverly from the men into whose power she had got. At the close of the trial, she left the Court with her young husband, leaving behind the memory of a very remarkable and a very fearless young woman."

THE END.